T0193940

Private Thoughts

Undivided Attention
Is the Most Romantic Thing
You Can Give to Anyone.

Anthony Green

authorHOUSE®

AuthorHouse™
1663 Liberty Drive
Bloomington, IN 47403
www.authorhouse.com
Phone: 1 (800) 839-8640

This is a work of fiction. All of the characters, names, incidents, organizations, and dialogue in this novel are either the products of the author's imagination or are used fictitiously.

Published by AuthorHouse 10/12/2017

ISBN: 978-1-5462-1180-8 (sc)
ISBN: 978-1-5462-1179-2 (hc)
ISBN: 978-1-5462-1178-5 (e)

Library of Congress Control Number: 2017915350

Print information available on the last page.

Any people depicted in stock imagery provided by Thinkstock are models, and such images are being used for illustrative purposes only. Certain stock imagery © Thinkstock.

This book is printed on acid-free paper.

As a child, I set and rearrange the world as I saw it threw writing and creating. I watched people and how they responded to each other in different types of relationships. None amazed me more than those that held simplicity of affection. The site of holding hands at time when people didn't publicly d display emotions because it was thought to be for the privilege of privacy. Never knew that would one day be me living out the things I've felt or learned by love.

Within learning the exposure to my feelings came out threw my pen. Now I place all that I am on display to be judged by, these are the things I've feared others who hear or see in me. My shame, my blame, me being misunderstood. This is a collection of thoughts inspired by life love and sex. All the elements of relationships you can enjoy. This book was designed to provoke and stimulate the part of my readers that feels passion for love. We all desire that one thing that sometimes we can't find in others, once it's found there is a nonstop urgency to contain and control the part of you that wants to let go.

It is here this mythical place of my endurance exceptionally sorting the seeds of my inherited fascinations of life. In this pixelated form jabbering at topics that no one understands. Men and women all try to place things into categories as we align them with how we think they should unite as one. All the things that holds solidity of substance disappear in the proof of romantic, casual & family relationships. There's no permanent breaking down of love and its boundaries subjectively enduring what we must, to be in its atmosphere.

The abstractions proletariat fights for its control trying to find the balance of its pleasure

All in which goes back to existence of mankind and its relationship form. The elements of attraction seeking hands that will touch him/her caress the salvaging pieces that may need resting.

Men and women verbally are known strangers searching for someone to verbalize discerning conceptions.

It's not ironic that two people meet exchanging signs of animalistic demeanor, it is only noted by the demanding phases of public laws of morality. The limits in laws of attraction have no direct or indirect choices of its findings. Seeing yourself describable as happily making decisions based totally off fitting emotions of panic. The racing of emotions allows reality to catch up with everything it has previously dismissed. Everything within both may be wanting or hoping this will change. Unfortunately, there's a part of each of us uncontrollably addicted to a need of lust, whilst the uttering words of others view and looking onto others causing a reaction calms and create balance.

No one is usually ready to settle down or ready to make relationship goals Investing time in people not on the same page as you open doors to differences of objectives, Building relationships out of imagination in which we think that is right pulling things from them that brings joy igniting consciousness. My intentions in my own life were to find a heart that's similar to that of my own. I've yet to see one close to humanity understanding these principles. What I've found and uncovered mostly seen in the best of us were the ugly flaws that exist hiding. We can't ignore the past of previous experiences. Our hearts never extinguish the pain we endure throughout life. We're invited to experience the pain of parents not hugging enough or not properly addressing the child in the right manner into the lives of other adults. This among many other things such as dysfunctional relationships with parents and those of our own peers, downpour of indifference of effects.

How we address our youth becomes the start of their relationship. This is the way they shall understand later in life.

Even if this understanding shall be found truthful we never love for values. We love for who others are willing to become outside of the arguments morality places us near. This way we get to escape what we will surely face in our questionable actions that are deemed irrelevant when two people lay together at the end of days. They'll enjoy the spiritual connections of how their souls entertains.

Joy always find gateways to different stories each uniquely detailed and refined as the last feeling driven by noticeable needs. Gasps scattering across grassy hills racing through the depths of valleys. All accessing combinations that release hands to uncover stimulating availability persuading what's envisioned.

In our existence, here on earth we should balance love alone with the hopes of faith that's accompanied by loneliness. Balancing these elements as if life is unchanging. You'll always be that one to feel the essence of moisture beneath skin intercepting one's thoughts. The altering of continuous exchanges of vows chemically moving and shaping

The limitless saga perpetuating truth of our own imaginations, all in which imitating life form.

Within this discernment I write these compilations of verses known as poem. The silent thoughts that rehearse everything it touches, understands, tastes, or frees the mind. There's a misconception about love and trust.

It is said that love don't suppose to hurt but people die daily leaving behind the pain of sorrow allowing others to grieve. Families in life proclaim love and affection often these connected relationships are broken. We are often reminded of people who have passed on, then there are those we lose in life. Some tend to overlook the complexities of others, simply to bound into the expressions of things they find invoking happiness. Their natures account for the basic reactions to the environment in which they share adapting to habits. All they've shared has been adjusted familiarity holding onto each other for the necessity of survival till death itself arrives.

Disappointment of trust is learned by the things we can't accept resulting in a loss expressing words that tend to break relationships. Trust alters relationships not with only one but everyone within the sound of the accuser's voice. Classification of mistrust, moral ethics & ability to demonstrate accuracy of word use.

Trust falls blind to recognitions lacking a form or position where man can point out and say. I hold the truth here and nothing changes it unless there's material or solid investment including demonstration of time. Most individuals don't begin to live until they've realized themselves operating fully as we've been created to conceive. Man's accountability to many emotions desiring love to be the most giving, receiving and appreciating what can't be recognized with simple words. If finding comfort from what's within causes injury to others they shouldn't be part of your life or have any type of placement in your life. It's nothing to be the best qualified human being, accounting for wellness, dignity and humanity. All these come with the understanding that we can't be mad at people for protecting who they want to remain. We must learn to stop asking people for what they are not capable of giving. Most aren't equipped with the knowledge of what they're entitled to give. More will develop their substance of how to give from the reserves of elder relationships limited to growth. Nothing is imagined creating happiness once the relationship has begun. Most imagine the idea vs actually giving thought to what will derive of being. The possibilities of growth lie within the small thing that impacts the receiver's choice. It's idea to constantly build within self, harmonizing the potential to increase the others growth. Depending on the principles applied and achieved through the youth stages of life, some characteristics will often leave most people by adulthood. They become judgmental and unfair even to themselves only seeking what was lost expressions from parents or trivial couples that may come to past their lives. Anyone that's willing to accept that no matter the race comes from broken understanding and will lead onto accomplished and beautiful relationships. Anxiety of wealth, spiritual, and lustrous desires, seating yourself with pride reduces stages of becoming lovers to desire each other. Love people the way you find them share pieces of yourself so they may choose if it's something that they're willing to use establishing a solid bond. The unraveling of you could break them, find what's worthy without denying them access due to your inability to see through them. Man can't always be what others expect. No one should try imitating what's not within or borrow the attitudes of others to address their own issues.

Our intellect can only serve us out of need exposing what may not be our truths. In building a relationship most default to sexual tendencies.

Monogamy is learned from the same concept in which forms the laws of morality. Maybe the same person said once you find a mate it's a good thing!! ...Who ever stated these things obviously never had a mate. Dealing with others and don't know some people it's pointless, or go through hell just trying to be in their life. Men /women it doesn't matter something's wrong with this picture. People that are dating going through hell trying to explain their positions...

Why convert life if it doesn't have to be. Most often people forget respecting others is a vital key in the success of their roles to maintain healthy relationship boundaries. It's hard to find people looking to manifest the appropriate relationships internally to produce happiness outwardly. Remembering to never develop a perception of one self. Allow others to determine what they've found. If you're acceptable to them do yourself the honors of not becoming friends with people unhappy within themselves.

When you're in love the only touch against your skin that matters the most is the one that you're loving. You may crave the attention of someone else you may pass, you may verbalize intentions to couple. None of it is an even exchange for that in which takes the place of the one you love. The most beautiful thing you'll ever see is your mate walking to you, their eyes only for you. Their intentions only involve you. Tasting their flesh becomes a lingering addiction in your mind. Listening to their conversation is all you want to hear followed by the sound of a zipper is the best sound you will ever imagine. Your thoughts begin to unravel at that moment blood begins to rush you start to visualize every sensation before it is conceived. Th eyes dilate, the tiny fibers of your hair responding resulting in chills. Sweat begin to leave the palms, the tongue becomes dry wanting to be wet, sexual sensations begin to move fears. Now you have the removal of blame resolving each other's problems by meeting the difficulty and restraints of each other's needs. Some will not always see the value of you, not even consider that greatness may lie beneath the walls of the exterior.

All efforts could be directed toward the highest level of mental efficiency. The repetitive thought process of what one has practiced constantly communicating the merits in which it predicts.

You can never return someone's joy after you have taken it, there are no Known remedies. A constructed amount of loyalty unlocks something so divine in another forming inspirational contagion of emotions.

The hardest quality of love is convincing someone who don't know love to return what it consists of. Simple things make love so Comfortably valuable you'd be willing to give up what you once considered valuable.

The insight of love's endless expression needs a little conversation to resolve all known preliminary remarks that strikes as foul. Resolutions should be so exclusive that you're able to make their small needs your objective for a daily task showing definite concerns. I think you should talk about the pain how it affects you what you need to move forward sometime pain exists in the smallest incidents. Most people hurt feelings without taking considerations of yours. It's healthy to speak of previous relations and their efforts to advance. No shame should be exorcised this helps you heal old scars, just because they're no longer in your life doesn't mean you don't still hurt.

Love has been an unseen universal element compensating to human feelings. Spilling what we determine purpose or attraction resulting especially what is fund of or idles. The significates of all life including those that are born. In all that's been analyzed applies things to construct systematic changes in lives of who or what's important to them.

When those things are met you're in tune. That's loving in the balance even when you're hurting to love. There's no love in a storm everybody's searching for a safe cover. Most are reaching to feel something within them arranging their emotions through stabilized trust, comfort, dignity, affection, and conversation followed by the joy they once felt (No one owns these emotions). They are passed on from one person to the next. For me it's breathing, seeing, touching, and exploring in terms with life the example of peace and spiritual growth producing things that reveals zest.

This mental conjunction in which we create for expression of loyalty. People search seeking attractiveness only to find it can't distinguish fact from fiction when it comes to trust. It's beginning is no greater than the center as it does near ending. Think of the beginning so when things are out of line you can return to offer miscellaneous methods of the same value. We rely on the word of trust just to say there's nothing more. From beginning to end we needed reasons to be cautious. This can be argued but think about it.

Many people don't come alive until they've concentrated within the reality of their physical world to produce things they've once envisioned. You should be yourself. Externally we force responsibility and accountability if others haven't lived and understand what life can give and take.

Love is that universal element that determines what's life, who's important to you.

The better you are the more people try to disgrace your character. You must distance yourself with those who just don't know being human isn't silenced by actions or the mouth. Be kind to all and accept their grace and love... People will never understand true meaning of being humble. Believe in your human spirit it connects to something greater than life itself

When you speak and people move either you're crazy or you're too sharp for their minds to comprehend difference or values.

Forever is time we lose sight, get comfortable and forget forever existed. For every forever, there's tomorrow to hope for peace and the will to survive

If there's no strength in the roots It wilts before it can produce anything as in great people. Strength is trained to rise above its teachers to create a better society of functional individuals. The objective of producing substance and charisma unconnected to its stems of growth will allow the production of power in everyone that applies themselves to reach maximum potential.

Powerless is taught, being trained is influenced by organizing a culture that listen to radios, televisions, read newspapers and social media, brain washing and dressing up how we should respond in different scenarios. All these things affect our emotional and social intelligence. Therefore, everyone is influenced by the powers of learning and adapting as others see fit. Wanting every individual conversation that they can connect with to advance and personal agendas.

The journey never advances beyond hurt and pain of theirs or other's mistakes. There are three faces that we all make happiness, sadness, and depression. Happiness is a journey within itself. It is the height of all emotions and gives you confidence of joy removing all distractions increasing your ability and ambition to do more than most would even understand. Sadness it an undeveloped relationship within one self. Disrupting esteem in conclusion it takes away anything that produces happiness. Depression is so many things its indescribable it exists in both.

This Power is calm, demanding, loving, and nurturing to its own body.

'I can't define the truth'
'I struggle'

My disposition I couldn't define with what I've considered experiencing as passion What I learned wasn't enough to give me provisions to douse the burning sensation of my experience.

I hadn't been turn on merely surviving worshiping the things we once embraced Emotions reacting generating appreciation for what intoxicates

Love was formed and made yet I couldn't define that part of me burrowed deep within the crevasse and quintessence hiding, from prospects silently moving

I begged of you, excavate me a definition emphasizing my use. Love lost. running races, crossing lines, cheating, boxing in the truth.

You've loved reading my boundaries being invaded smiling appreciating my thoughts.

Amplified to manifest my humble inhabitants, communicate sensual crashes Of filthy chattels. Atoms swooning secretions sprouting in your veins selfishly in its own passion.

Conception blending standards without control, appearing only to the reaction of this chemistry. Shall you experience orgasms and complexities of beating pluses needing to find consummation in your seams. Eagerly clinching with the sweating of hands the loud beats of your heart heard within. Twitching of fingers pondering should you free yourself of this sticky irritable feeling.

The warmth forcing utters penetrating violate throbbing.

Arches in your skin appear leaving you victimized gazed in heat with only choices. How else could we constitute endless devotion that resonates us sharing?

I loved everything that had no feelings for me.

I crave what can't be given.

To blame myself was the rule I pretended to follow.

The efforts I've taken to provide, protect, please and love had no effect directly.

Often times I never needed love just wanted to give what was never given.

Within these things I felt it hard to say what love really means to me.

Lose control feel the missing pieces shower.

Put on your sexy underwear let them take warmth

Fix yourself a drink pour a little for me taste the pleasure of what you imagine

Pick up your cell phone take snapshots till you're turned on.

You must understand I'm the reason you're in heat moisture

I want to be there in your flesh since I can't play with it until you're a mess.

Send me those snapshots you know I like that.

I was thinking of you this morning "freaky things"

Loving you isn't always what it seems. Take a picture to apologize for all you can't do, amongst everything let me see them pretty fingers in you. This is the prescription to my pleasure. Beyond many things you'll become Rx-rated this perception for intended use of exhales of warmth beneath your feet glaze eyes gaze to find mine. An arrangement of simple succulent taste of your toes. Hissing musicals to tremble your feet. The charm of splendid lines wet and glistening. Galant desire exposing intentions to feel teeth nudge over nails engage to this heart beating in your feet.

Impulses confirmed pleasurable moments pondering similar to those walked upon sand

leading to waters of climaxing oceans. Securely embraced in my hands intoxicated by your flesh. The brown of your skin those beautiful chocolate drops. My intentions are to heat and melt the puff and blow until you're covered on the walls. Soft objections from minor slips of the tongues longing to lay gasping with hands in the air awkwardly satisfaction renewing vitality. The hidden cries modified to drift about. Impressive sound when life is silent poetry and pain love and joy coiled beneath diverse confidence. Equally capable of cultivation of ideas yet I'm vulnerable to voids and deficiencies. The restlessness of breaking chains grooming myself to stand firm with an attentive nature. To challenge my anger suspending responses of arrogance adjusting to life without pretending.

Developed the anger breaking character within myself, the part that needs acceptance suffering of self-pitying. Genuine happiness nothing left to chance, I find myself in dark places idling for days sometimes even months waiting to be held. I'm the brush in your chalice the one to intertwine with the paint on my brush It's you that my clashes understand, its impressions are so wonderfully displayed. I'm a man yearning just to be in control over your strokes.

You're the decor splattered on my walls most will never know of this feel. My approach to catch the fallen stars when the skies cry out to infuse with the undercoat. Together we watch as the dyes brighten as the sun set enhances as it repositions

I perceive you spreading the rainbow across the sky 2 characters you and I.

You're the spatter that start dreams arrays of colors gazed upon only what's to be sodden in a fascinating exhibition Painting the flushes of everything wrapped around me it's to my understanding. Plants never bloomed without a seed with the simplest drop of water and a grain of earth. It only takes a tiny fraction of touch to change views and we can share everything that has bloomed. I saw and felt parts of you before you enter a room you resembled

fine tunes of petaled flowers setting under the sun in the afternoon. Paint dripping it occurs to me everything falls as the mist between a kiss similar to the color of lipstick. I've desired the finer details after I dipped leaving my marks.

Once we are combined where searches began there's simplicity inside the perfection of these lines.

The maturity in what others related to as distress ion lay waiting for me on any canvas of your choosing. Conclusions of paint en-synced beautiful in us there we recreate heaven and earth,

with everything in it, from the beginning to the end. It's the substance inside of the paint I exercise trust exemplifying what love looks and feels like. The change of everyone's emotions. while the moon awaits the two to be drawn and painted in satin sheets.

'Paint don't dry'

I'd choose you beneath a wet sea on black sand. We were validated at conception the first drop and every stroke from different wounds. If I continue I'll have your heart wrapped around me wet all in that deep blue. Perfection can't be rushed to dry even for a little touch up. What more can a brush be without the artist to arrange his style before he lays it down. Sit back and

Imagine a universe where souls moving clouds Feelings scream out loud, silence imitating whispering thoughts & Fear didn't exist Loves only meaning was saved kisses, if only caressing was caring and sharing was burying shattered pieces. Would everyone hide from us if escaping negativity was ecstasy Positively whilst granting you passionate feelings to the 3rd degree. My reality of any wish would be for everyone to see love inside us Trust everything without measures lust would lead to strong marriages May the epiphanies of presence undress you Roses will orchestrate perfect moments Sounding off symphonies Loves only condition can be found in your company Words undefined in relationships Perfection was aged beauty Death birth religion Trouble invent new ideas Seasons restored feelings again.

Sex is lying next to you to feel multiple orgasms lasting the whole night threw. Just in case the champagne loses its fizz the norm would be the strokes of your hands moving down my spine. Keeping the candles lit would cancel storms. Sex is lying next to you feeling your breath against my skin, listening to the sound of your voice, those gentle touches you deliver, my hands moving over your bent spine, indulging in your aroma, I can't get enough and it's why we can recreate what last the whole night threw.

My goddesses I shall fulfill desires you may have. Love or lay down for your causes. Enjoying your sensitivity for myself You'll never love yourself as much as I.

My truth of depth for u Whatever love you may have experienced I have more to give, I have more to teach, I have more for you to learn. I give up freely all control of myself just to combine convolutions of savagery and the beauty of nature itself.

I deserve to have you in my world I intend to rob you of everything all that you can't give all that's hidden every moment desired from touch to taste I'm the thief that will face you without a mask or gun. Telling you what to give while you offer it freely begging for me to take control and whip you.

On Your Knees!

No shirt pants or shoes breaking all of your untamed restraints.

Tossing pillows ripping sheets damaging the walls above the bed.

Make sure someone come running to rescue you but can't get in

Gagged and tied until I set you free I promise to rob you of innocence.

I'll leave you with only joy and happiness I'm taking all your love I'm selfish no one deserves it but me...

To treat you so kind, so gentle very sweet to have you to wonder if being robbed is worth breaking free

"Old Cliché"

It's me she dreams of, simple and plain text hot and sweaty wet

Gazing in her eyes on foreign sand pointing at beautiful things holding hands.

Lost and abandoned weaken by love my heart torn and shredded

Pieces placed on two ends of the earth running trying to catch both opening at the right time.

Screaming love are you here I need you each way I been running I miss what is meant to be

Love why have you chosen me is this the way life supposed to be

One end there was birth to beauty the other end was death of love

Candles lit over an incredible dish waits love pouring out the juices that remain.

The other there's peace

A smile at a dancing within a conversation that's endless eyes lit

Ready to trace the light in which it was created in the middle

There's hooks, chains, and rope mounting me to an old maple tree.

Running around chasing what I couldn't catch, even what I saw couldn't be touched.

It's amazing the way you made me love you its clever how shit comes back to bite you.

No spit for lines just quality time

Long conversations no bitching and aggravation it's funny it began as something to do to satisfy time

However, love was new to you even though you where cold hearted didn't know it was about to hit you with a warm switch

Went from fuck a negro to he's my hero. Mild conversation & breaking you off daily

Enchanted notes of heart ache and forsaken love obvious mistakes.

Poetic views of different estates encouraged by hardship and broken by faith.

I pour out my soul for as long as it takes

Heated walking streets cold as ice, fighting off the wind knocking on doors looking for my friends.

Double take double look imagine me balled in a corner with a nose freeze.

Counting on my hands the amount of time I've said please

Ambition drop lost left behind morals changed all I couldn't began to erase.

In the sunset, I stare for trust the hate within is always too much

Light that guides the hand that moves is the light that guides the orbit of the moon the gravity of touch holds man

From dust so cherish the days you expire with lust and challenge

What are the odds to complete a goal because my temperature rises to ease the cold.

Misplaced hands missed holds her truth real feelings given to you

"I haven't loved but it maybe you" words delivered pressed in her feelings

"If I'm what you need you can have me" strokes aiming to feed your success

"You give me life all I want is joy next you can have all you can keep.

The touch to her body was empty and cold filled with breezes across her ass cheeks.

Only the throbbing of action waiting on hands prior to loving her dangling waiting to be a love toy.

Aching to see what was felt

Touches stopping at reaching the inner soul to pull her face feeling an exuberant kiss crawling over the wetness of her lips.

Eyes lock close smell the freshness of favorites.

Mental scribbles of scratches made with her mouth open. Clinched fists Spiritually invaded by epiphanies of bliss, as bodies cling to each other's up and down.

Sweat to be dampened with his tongue chased to cracked places, to be suctioned out with his mouthpiece.

Kicks to begin without controls of how they may end after biting of flesh spreaded ideally from legs to neck.

Gagged, choked, hog tied, anything but sex love connecting souls loving moments racing to win bets.

Beautiful to believe that he gathered her truth but missed it all with lies claiming love when it was less than sex.

Hard up for a body to experience didn't listen to the words it was trying to teach.

Waving of romance danced in mental notes leaving her to fend for love the most.

Beautiful eyes hide what's missing inside.

I watch you wetter from dried excuses

why you haven't experienced ecstasy?

You're perfect maybe I'm mistaken excepting what you haven't earned.

Learning what love isn't, leaves no room for my reason or another to love what's shattered.

Unfixed, unclear, unclaimed, unsatisfied understanding what you believe will work out

without words wondering what he needs to claim, control clarifying his craving for other women.

Had it been me I'd love looting loud lusting languages lasting longer licking like love left leaving you

Screaming for your fix while beautiful petals silhouette over waters overflowing trusting in this arranged moment.

These flickering shadows take shape in my mind.

Our wet bodies dried in flames of ecstasy

She's chasing my thoughts to extinguish the burden of raptures.

We listen to familiar sounds of pleasure

inviting simulation to witness wall falls relocating to your final inherited orgasms

Tell me What is it you can't say

Last night I was drunken gasping simultaneously of air, the moisture of wetness,

Powerful indulging taste, sweat rolling off my face.

The water left over of the bathe wine still sating weakness remain in my legs, bruised of thrusting

intoxicated pounding.

Scratches unexplained pulled from the drunken of love mixing flavors

high on poetry slurs of my words slowly explaining to my drunken self

Drizzling thoughts of eruptions flowing down to earthquakes of volcanic explosions...

Expressive smiles solitudes my eyes to close gazing into the deepest void conceived in my soul.

Scorned to scream at my heart as it returns a whispering you will love.

I've no sympathy for what's demeaning inside your life, what gives you reasons to close the part that should be open for me.

The increase of desire to never want for a love that's snatched away you've carelessly over looked.

What good does it do to miss something I can't have I'm abandoning myself replacing love with voids

I'll keep you in my heart so I'm never without.

Life goes in full circles who knows maybe one day know this is my heart.

I've never loved anyone with this madness overlooking my own gratification to happiness.

I loved you, filled you with me and an unknown certainty lost beyond the reaches of bliss.

It will take some time to let go I could have loved u all my life. Had not been for the other thing's that came into play.

Allow your eyes to follow the room door open it, chat with me about your day tell it to me again and again, say it stop that.

Feel my bites," I want that "slaps on your ass.

Take That Off!

Undress the rest.

You may not know how much I like this rubbing on you, can you feel that?

Looking in your eyes, look at me once more. I want you to see you naked, skin to skin I need all of you.

Kisses from your lips to your hips in your own words. Define reasoning for 2 nipples in my face can you see me tasting the ridges? Limitless to see optimistic essences of a future we both seize!

Please with the liberty of crawling hands mysteriously stiffing and fondly thoughts

Pieces that I should have of you subconsciously in love empty of everything but words to offer

Violently explaining the blushes on your cheeks. Reality finally hits me all the words of my choosing couldn't save me. I was swimming without a lesson.

Ships sail by people aligned the shores smiling laughing, holding hands

Sharing their modesty opinions of experiences.

I on the other hand unable to float casted away, anchored and weighed down.

Thoughts can't expand passing seaweed with the unpleasantry of sea gulls flying over shitting on me.

What I'd give for someone to grab my hand, (rescue me).

Resuscitate me while I live, hold my head place lips willingly to my face.

Hold me as I'm near death I lay smiling because I get to look into your eyes in need of rescue.

Bathe my heart in these waters I can see through the blue waves.

Love me as if it's my last breath cry give me your pain for my happiness

I'm drowning going down suspended with my eyes closed. Thinking of the way it used to be.

"Before my death" let me remember us holding hands, kissing on this very sand.

Talking remembering how we were made for one another.

You where the light in the house that guided me. Now I look and the light shines no more.

The house stands with old poetry I wrote with expressions of love.

Now pages just blow out the window of hidden cries modified to drafts

Impressive mental sounds when life is silent poetry and pain lovely joy coiled beneath diverse confidence.

Equally capable of cultivation ideas yet I'm vulnerable to voids and deficiencies.

The restlessness of breaking chains grooming myself to the stand within my attentive nature.

All in which challenges anger suspending responses of arrogance adjusting to life without pretending, developing hate within myself, the part of myself needs acceptance the suffering of self-pitying.

Aside from genuine happiness there's nothing left to chance.

One day I found myself running after pages trying to read reminding myself what we held on to.

The grace of your smile lived within me it's a complimentary to everything we believed.

Spider webs align the ceilings, echoes bounce off the walls.

Saddened with my conviction of the truth, I knew one day I would lay lifeless upon this very shore.

Little did I know you would be passing me by watching me drown.

My loud hidden cries modified to drift about the impressive sound when life is silent.

Poetry and pain love and joy coiled beneath distinct conviction.

I fall victim to her prayer changing in whom shall I give these contemplated advantages of feelings

I've dismissed circulating ideas with no indicated reasons to boast upon frequent philosophy.

Happiness of my affection combine mystically kneeling drunkenly chills in my flesh.

I've randomly explored millions of theories spoken in untranslated versions.

Over time the truth is harder to bare yet it does not matter for now it's important to (think).

I've broken hearts for less than love I've been dominated by the cruelty of intentions to feel what wasn't there.

Misleading erections to run after the excellence of the meaningless fluff, and the divined

cliffs of her thighs. Absolutely no interest knowingly we're both to suffer an obvious ending.

Discussions of failed attempts left to be the company of a guy unnamed. Why would my non

concerned ego contemplate ideas of what was intended to neglect? That would leave you to miss the uplifting of happiness, the purity of habits creating ecstasy. The abandonment of a permanent love filled with a definite resolution. "So far from the truth to a degree" No one should be spared the ideal invitation to a higher quality poetic to the nature of my soul. She who finds use with my great many words to be romanced by reminisces significant to possess fearlessly.

Never a time to be without discipline to give acts of submissions, With thoughts so far from open legs but the worship of all the actions seemingly weakened to the external view while strengthening the internal depths of me. Gathering ideas to change my innocence to feel only guilt of our amusement. Despite all affection has never claimed the mountain of my failed attempts to love. The price of love visualizes what it means to crave a satisfying conversation words drawing blueprints to climax of serenity in emotions busting condemned barricaded walls of trust. The combination of time trusting all in which I've spent commencing to find love.

My ideas started to redirect where to we found mated hearts. Or am I to believe ideas where not of my reality or my presence but the past of my feelings. "For now, I find myself trying" to permanently resolve my feelings. Have I loved you not more in the beginning, inferior to as I do at this moment. Would it be in between that we've invented to imagine our best similarly to my past? Flames burn no reason why you should believe ashes haven't heat or flames not exist.

I'm convinced for now flamed ash should not be touched allow them to burn. Love is incompatible inconsistent to when and where I began to feel. Can you account for that moment without words spoken. Was your heart engaged at the exchange of words. Thus, this wouldn't support my heart when I set eyes upon you. Naturally I'm confused had I began to be fair to myself or should I feel cheated. A foolish heart had perceived love existence yet it wasn't a valid exploration for my feelings. A contradiction lonely as it has always been Why should I believe what I remember if it's different from time. My imagination has been extended to dwell at length.

Here I sit remaining trying to provoke a revival of feelings. What constitutes a primitive affair without mixing where you or I loved one another. Certainly, hearts go through emotional emptiness how would we distinguish if there was anything to offer? The remains are opinions we introduced to restore time in between to be investigated. In all of your doing most often times it is all forgotten there's a process to everything that is done. Out of most of what I recognize are those that aim to increase their economics of living. I don't know about most the journey isn't fighting or, struggling, or even overcoming. Relating to meeting me daily with a kiss, women be pampered Digest our (relationships) work on this efficient love. Attempt the process of how we treat each other things brought forward loving, erases the bases of reasons to feel anything else. Feed of me passionate ideas practice depending on nothing outside of feelings to increase intimacy. Spoil yourself of a beautiful life this could be the truth of why our bodies intertwine. Watch as the rousing of my thoughts separate my fingers to fall upon the faces of prints. Marrow begin stirring in my bones blood burning in the fire my spirit moves farther away so it can't hear the groaning sounds of the souls. The yelling of vibration to be heard in unfamiliar galaxies with the physical flesh beyond its reach.

Within one glimpse there was something to be seen as beautiful. Unveiled before my eyes was everything that was hidden in the laughter of love. The smile of an angel walking right before my eyes within my presence. The silence of my thoughts wandered rearranged the past, future, and present. I even saw myself die a tearful death leaving her behind. The tears rolling down her face there I stood in my spiritual form right before her I wept. I extended out to taste her tears sweetest thing ever to my lips. The voice I couldn't get enough of cringed by draining me of my spiritual presence. There in present time sweat poured through the palms of my hands.

Thinking to myself stay calm introduce yourself I just couldn't find the words.

She chuckled and our souls united conversations lasted for hours knowing things

neither of us knew we were interested in. Nothing was more flattering than

wanting more.

My eyes required more than my hands where allowed settling for simplicity of touches.

Nights past thoughts erupted words that where no longer enough. We wanted to lock breath, intermingle the magic of the sparkle within our soulful ubiety. Our feet requested walks upon shores near clear azure waters. Hands required us to cradle each other locking opportunities in arms....Still we bicker about love who floats deeper beyond the abyss. Why our solar systems aren't rained upon. Too much sun when everything is perfectly aligned

How many ways do I need to define myself. How many times do you need to hear my truth. I've loved, trusted, offered new meanings to spit this reality into a broken mentality. Eyes watered because you saw what was left. Truth is you were never there. "For now, I find myself trying" to permanently resolve my feelings. Have I loved you not more in the beginning? Inferior to as I do at this moment.

Would it be in between that we've invented to imagine our best?

Similarly, to my past flames burn no reasons why you should believe ashes haven't had heat or flames never existed. I'm convinced for now, flamed ash to not be touched let it burn. Love is incompatible inconsistent to when and where I began to feel. Can you account for that moment without words spoken? Was your heart engaged at the exchange of words. Thus wouldn't support my heart when I set eyes upon you. Naturally I'm confused had I began to be fair to myself or should I feel cheated. A foolish heart had perceived love existence yet it wasn't a valid exploration for my feelings. A contradiction that stood alone. Why should I believe what I remember if it's different from time? My imagination has been extended to dwell at length. Here I still sit remaining idle trying to provoke a revival of feelings. What constitutes a primitive affair without mixing where you or I loved one another. Certainly, hearts go through emotional emptiness how else would we distinguish, if there was anything to offer.

The remains are opinions we introduced to restore time in between to be investigated. The combination of time in which I've spent commencing to find love.

My ideas started to redirect where to we found mated hearts. Or am I to believe ideas where not of my reality or my presence but the past of my feelings. Would it be in between that we've invented to imagine our best? Similarly, to my past, flames burn for no reason why you should believe ashes haven't heat or flames not exist. The splendor of radiant beauty chases what I want most. Seeking external use of what I may find to be good lustrous and serene. Why should I not reveal the concealed power of your fertility. Considering this has consumed my tiring thoughts. I can't do to myself what I want to share. Each shred of dignity should be ripped away. I only desire an opportunity to expand my significant. How confined should we be to penetrate deliverable sweet orgasmic oceans. Strides to capture the winds of breathes. To dock lips near the end of passages to pleasure. I admit I cannot satisfy my thirst of your salty water. Nor shall I restrain arms or legs leaving you to chase your soul. I've chosen to find the part of you attached hindered fearless I didn't know. In my search, we were already connected. There you were holding my fibers within your fingers ready to pull me closer. "I'm now a mere understanding of what you recognize as pieces." You've clothed my will! Unmistakably baring warmth to a soul that only makes happiness greater than the reality. "I'm eloquently desiring " the softness of your skin. The secret of a comfortable beginning. "Let it dress my nakedness" Bring your phenomenal tools to tighten up drippings. Study my chemistry, master breaking up my elements. Find the basics for our existence, in shared space educate me on loving you. I'm to drown within this body, without you holding on to me.

Help me breath! Resuscitate me!

I feel myself slipping away. I can't exchange anything in less value that's worthy of living… If she never hears or understand I have a collection of only words. A few belongings to how I see her to be Cursed with my blessings. My blessings her excuse to not believe what she has heard. If I'm to lay and think I'd lye to recollections of memories. None are stored just a momentarily Hello. Then it's goodbye left outside my reality only similarities. We blink and we lose what we won. Only if she heard my dreams she'd give me the things I ask her to bring. Carry my heart pick up my soul pack my spirt cover me beneath your emotions. Hide me keep what you can use I'm a handful but a handy tool Never knew myself until someone told me how they thought I should be. I couldn't live until a part of me died. Suffered complications of acknowledgments without feelings of success. Sprit lost and wondering Doing what everyone else do walk, awhile fall off. Claim the love of my maker when I didn't trust, my feelings Biblical terms or didn't know him at all. Chased empty thoughts of verses that was repeated. Thy shall thou shall not. Learned words without cleansing my soul. Gave away my depths to keep the parts of people that wasn't no good to me.

Listen to what they needed to keep me. The wise lives alone trust only what he sees Nothing about what he believes truth doesn't belong to his imagination. The lost was forgotten past left to reform futures. I haven't properly introduced myself I am trapped in feelings Holding onto your hopes of love lending your strength desires that's haven't been inhabited. I'm cringed sensible in bed unaccompanied by needs unsure what I was looking at until I saw shoes underneath the laced panties this was a night of love what would lead to be a lifetime of memories. Strains of hairs underneath my grooved fingertips. The friction of mixed moisture on our skin creating love potions. Eyes cutting the room in delirious motions, I imagine my hands-on ceilings painting masterpieces with your legs wrapped around the back of me. These misunderstood languages in which we speak. I can hear you calling out for love in every moan and the clinching of my flesh.

I whispered ecstasy within every thrust there we have to battle warm wet juices taking what's mine. Nothing please me more than watching you wiggling trying to escape crawling across desert of white sheets. In these small valuable minutes of romance striking the hearts of many simultaneously. One smile behind the next never had I thought loving anyone with this amount of emotions would have been enough I've only considered sex. I often said I never needed love just wanted to give what was never given. I find it hard to say what's needed to escape the madness that's got me pulling away your clothes. DAMN that lace on the bed got methinking, seeing your shoes by the door now hands are sweaty wet. If I'm to get away with undressing you completely who's to say I'll find the love needed to include my happiness and use it as a tool. I'd expect you to surrender! I can get use to you being pampered digesting our (relationship), working towards this efficient love attempt our process of how we treat each other.

Things brought forward love erases the bases of reasons to feel anything else. Feed of me passionate ideas practice depending on nothing outside of feelings to increase intimacy. In our existence, we must balance love in hopes that it never changes its feel the texture of moist intercepting thoughts that exchanges a continuous flow of vows. The limitless saga perpetuating truth of our imagination imitating life form therefore. Love is carelessly given even if it hurts until you can understand the pain of the voids with you or the persons. "We" continue to give in an unselfish manner in faith that we are healing another through the God given power unexplained. As we feel in our hearts we become what's felt, often finding every reason not to love but to have reasons to push others away. As we all have the intoxicating awareness to wait patiently. No one should have authority to make changes in your life or arrange your emotions people should be powerless. Unnecessarily rested needing attention then she walked in.

A slender sexy conversational piece "come join me in my room."

She sat

She wanted nothing less only more of what she'd have of me. She wanted me to abduct my voice, change my mind and give pleasures in parts to my body I couldn't have given. I was left in a situation she opened to me all her passionate affections. The spiritual connections in a room undressing and leaving clothes on my floor, high out of her mind. Locked with my spirit intoxicated of love riding me. Fingers locked our exchanges the "ooohs" and awws!!

These tunes spoken only in poetry. Something so unique experiencing drizzling skeets lost clinched between her knees. Her eyes rolling, she couldn't stop them from gazing at my body art, she painted herself in my heart. She had drawn herself as my lover writing respectfully fluent notes of profound verses instilling lustrous panic in my deepest memory. My drawbacks were the heart outside was locked she had the key to place herself inside of the warmth of the chamber walls. She had questioned herself but hadn't realized I had thrown away the last key. Now I'm without anything to give to another no sweet talk, no unconditional promises Just me taking back all the sweet things pleasantly spoken. Even those futures expressions that would lock my love She looked upon my wing to spread, wondering of the beast that had infiltrated within me I gave her my love and a feather to write with when she felt blue. I don't know if she understood the love she wrote increased my appetite, endlessly for the pieces of her I'd never see.

'So, she writes'

Love investments, sexual establishments of ecstasy roses grown on the surface of moons

Bursting flames from the sun made the love we've shared become cold,

To much time in a galaxy of our stars sitting looking to see which one she has named for me.

Love and spiritual souls locked in the folds or hiding from the winner not willing to acknowledge you gambled the truth. Love never allowed me to cut in. Left behind only hearts that seamlessly to comfort the outside of windows without openings to let the freshness of air flow in.

Foggy memories admiring trees blossoming resentment of green leaves, observation as parts of you wither away I can't tell you why love give smiles that will soon be erased trouncing these separated dimensions against a shrine among flowers. In the first season, I learned that it wasn't easy finding the inclination to move pass what I could define as love.

My eyes released waters that was clear as rain it came so heavy breaking me free of positive definitions. Who can say they've loved you more than me, I've loved you more than the creator himself. Nothing could have been better it all resembles the lines where the clouds meet the sky, the beginning of the first spark of lightning and the dust of the last darkness. The first seed of earth, the first drop of water. "This love is the making of atoms." Don't tell me you love the ground I walk on in the face of defeat I ran up. Mountains dissolve as I climb and climb, scared scrape and bruised look down upon the valleys. Built temporary shelter looking ahead checking gloves, mittens, and hardware of rope. With nothing to give others wasn't lucky enough to find what I couldn't outline myself.

Sunlight glowing through the tress shadowing my thoughts, dancing on river beds running across waving at what's left. Painted pictures revealed everything without the meaning. I can't define love I'd love to say it's on your lips that stick out colored and soft. Maybe it's in the arms that reach around the back of me opening faces of hands rubbing the thread over smooth skin.

My soul measured memories provocatively believed to communicate the cost of any objectively displayed 4play. My shoulders await intercourse linking the effects of your wishes to the prolonged wondering desiring affection raging through your hands.

I should have

Less than a minute I fought it out the fiery of my thrusting tears. All my possessions of loves certainties plunged out the delicate affection prolonged striping me of all desires presumably needed.

To think I'm to give up what was executed through mustard courage extinguished moments no longer in the shadows. My eyes fixed to stare at memories of your beautiful hands the exquisite softness of their touches beneath manicured nails to think how much have I loss of you.

I'm at a disadvantage without your slow smiling gaze pledging with my soul. I've no place of saved hope it's impossible to carry around these aching words wondering of my negligence as these tears trickle down. Flowers received all I'd poured shrub the leaves soothing a long-awaited thirst. The gravel arouses the ground cracked of swallowed roots recovering my firm intentions to grow us. Now it's pedals inherits what I don't trust myself to keep all I'd imagined.

A wife left laying on my bed exhausted unhurried ready to receive the wind howling beneath the chirping of birds. Longing for one touch carefully placed under the purple satin sheets.

I'm selfishly wanting you stretched syncing every word you'll moan. Force every finger you have into my flesh, close the gates to see anything but the darkness of my life. Fasten muscles around portions I should be pressed to spill your waters close enough for me to taste. Fight for us within this room rip away sheets to get me to stay. Not just living to stay till the end I find myself living to find that place we began. What if I hadn't said a word I would have written until the sun came up. Time would have stood still holding on to my words allowing them to birth new beginnings. Feel their conception, what if I had said more? I wonder if it's true what they say?

We're able to rearrange life as we see fit. I'd leave everything to chance. The only thing I'd leave the same would be the enlightenment of your smile it captures my whole heart within the gentleness of touches. Your hands outline life's softer moments thoughts settling as it was a mist above the ground shaping and nurturing yielding seeds. I want nothing more than to live somewhere near arrangements of only your beautiful thoughts. I've smiled many days without happiness. Now I can change all of that starting with trusting you to be the person locked away never asked to see life. Before we, there was the oceans of tears trying to pour into each other. On the cliffs prayer went out and returned you. Would it have made a difference?

A reflection misunderstood construed to explain born to find things others deny.

Therefore, tell the truth we belong to life I can't image life if it belongs to us.

We'd separate the scars light hides its beauty. We would toss the sun up just to be snatched back down rotate it until it breaks.

Somehow, we'll freeze the wind and drain oceans looking for traces of a God. Nothing is honest about man we'd see a face sneak and rearrange what once was excepting to us.

We'd lie about the truth, imagine what you'd change if your me extra thighs, different face, longer hands, some would steal success resting and removing those they can't stand. What a mess we'd make.

A house holds 6 to 7 men and many women because we'd keep the ones we love.

Somehow balance would be lost nothing would be sane. No flowers or spring clouded arrangements, no sign of life amongst insects taken away the joy of life. Artist with nothing to paint, poets without words, marriages with no reasons tears for everyone and everything.

Mysterious beliefs including sex in exchange to be saved. Wait maybe someone would chain God shame him and blame him for the beauty of life we go through. Old people would wander the streets screaming and shouting wanting death. This is the world we'd live in if we had control. What if we continue to communicate would you be able to stop?

What if I'm the one to show you life would I become part of your life?

Walking across dirt roads through the fields of tall grass I saw dreams. They were clouded with my imagination. Justifying what was in reality, with magic sticks building tents erasing myself of the future poverty rate. The nap on my head was pretended that of a king after introduced to King the kid Tut. Never will I forget the amazing excitement to venture off to sleep. It was there, I found peace placing myself on different pages. Days of strong winds I placed myself on the ground searching through different theories back down facing the sky. Watching the skies expand and change shape thinking of what God would be. Who was he, how he came about, or how his thoughts where arranged. Were his parents proud to see what he may of us? More so to see the objects in the sky socializing with each pointing placing wishes beneath.

Nights would pass with grandad would sing and play his guitar the melodies took me about the trees eyes closed a boy lost in dashed notes. It wasn't until I heard the word potential I opened use to use words and make different views …My first poem. I'm a man lost inside a little boy. A boy trying to be a man.In this divinity of time it is everything, falls from grains of sand holding dominion over lovers measuring the silence of words within distances exchanging soft raptures. Each lingering creating an evolution instant gratification of what the truth holds as the test of time. Still I wonder if it can be held near leaves beneath pecan trees. May just maybe it hide in glasses of wine. That's theonly moment it spins and shifts, lapses causes us to forget of its vice during this miserable occasion. Making us all prisoners and slaves to sleep only if we aren't chosen to be staggering fools. We're all running hopelessly trying to be saved. Virgins looking and feeling it's, presence knowing at some point we'll be rejected of its journey till it's no more.

All accuse time of hardship and duties unfair taking what we love giving what never last. Statues stand and watch people cry burying it young showing no expressions not sharing one word knowing it's time will come no escape not even in dreams. It is here right now my forever show me where time rest and awake. I could only hope it accompanies love and grace.

The clarity of dying men in the rough beholding gold splendors reacting to glimmers of gems color. Time is a prejudice king killing all things its idolized like stars in the sky. Saving its reasons why we wish upon each, awaiting tides to revitalize youthful memories it humbles walks on beaches excavating fossils believed to have discovered what time never tells. Intimate secrets shared with the wind whispering as it lay down beside trees turning the world to thieves taking what could've been done in a day's labor stretching it past months even years. It takes our sweat dry it gives it back (condensation) to sweat some more. While our tears fall time embraces us.

As it teaches strength the father of all pain. Our inheritance of resources narrator & author of responsibility.

Behold it belongs to god even he belongs to it in a sense from nothing comes everything to end everything and still never ends. Time hides in places for no one to find. We rearrange, separate, chase, cheat and race. It's never been found only mistaken replacement traces. It is our pimp, in time we all bust nuts from corner to jumping in and out of cars doing whatever it takes to feed ourselves alone with our family members as well. Each praying for a little more junkie with habits strung out. With no voice, I'll scream out into the world hoping you'd hear the passion in my voice. Hear my silence when no words are said just the look expressing what I love. Place your hand over my heart wait for it to stop so I can begin to live again. I share with you my life and every way I find new to love. Those treasures buried deep within me sit under rainbows created by tears of loving you. I remember the beginning writing letters now you're the muse of my poetry.

Men will learn love women will learn of a love that exists so deep within me.

Maybe I'm in love with the first smile hoping to glimpse or relive it again. One thing for sure god gave me you I've known before we were about to be united in verses. General conversation appreciating you being a woman may be a little flattering. But it shouldn't be taken as flirtatious. I'll teach yourself what you need before seeking what you want. In saying that all men say you look good or enjoy the way you move or enjoy your company. But those are just meager things. Those things leave you to question what is it about me...If he finds distinctive things such as what I said earlier.

I said that because when I met you although you didn't know me you gave enough attention to consider maybe I was a nice person or highly flirtatious. So not the case however you were easy to laugh and showed a great deal of interest in what I was saying. When I looked up everyone in the store noticed our conversation. You never made any judgment or asked a single question gracefully I excepted your friendship. Those are qualities men search for a woman who's ready to listen and bound he can teach her to different levels and respect her while doing so. All women want to know themselves and I believe it's harder to find if you haven't excepted all of yourself. I don't mean that person in the mirror I mean that what's locked inside unleashed.

And it's fine just try to find out as much as you can about any man you deal with because those are the things that make or break you don't allow your feelings to decide. Know for sure and always talk to him as a friend before entering a relationship. If he's having problems with other women he doesn't deserve your body. That's period! If you're unsure the type of man hangs out with him in a group judging him by his friends is ok but judge him according to what he's willing to give up having you. Just because you're in a relationship doesn't put u first.

Understand it's not just the man that defines your position. Sharing information that's part of deciding where to get comfortable at before moving forward.

I am grace
I am tears
I am the light
I am what most feared
I'm feared by black and white
I fear myself
In an anointed presence
I've lost my way but I am here.
There's an angel with a hand
full of petals awaiting

One day you'll look for me
my voice will have silenced
My eyes will have closed on
all the memories of yesterday
Will be blocked away beneath lids

Of a corpse

I wouldn't have thought today
would have been the day.
Tomorrow is unseen presently

I speak from within.

I was having a moment wanted to be left alone it was she reluctantly providing the grace of her presence.

I was delightfully obliged to pour my exemplary promises I once held onto letters finding my way through pictures to feel passions unburned, Words filled the silent hallway of my heart.

I Shedd tears at the thoughts of your virginity spreading into the atmosphere. I wanted her unbroken untouched even by my hands. Allow my heart to bleed for her touch.

Fingertips to trace her face to straighten her brows Glimmering bliss at her arches shall her eyes close at my fragrance while kisses left upon her nose. How often will I think of her lips each line lingering within my delightful Wishes. As I prepare for raptures to appear at a connection.

I could pull away and know the sun shall be brighter seeing heaven in her eyes. I tremble at a glance knowing one must live this life connected to the sorrows of echoes. Wanting and missing What is rest within her. I've not enough words, not

enough love, not enough joy, not enough belief. Ghost of my romantic imagery tasting, touching, laying, whispering energy transferred of intimate conversations sparks tenaciously wanting to taste softness of skin. Starting nail by nail gathering and releasing A delicacy, enjoyed rejuvenation changing my intellectual understanding of romance collectively changing and challenging the course of my impulses. I'm awake dead to the world dreaming of you and me.

Society thinks I should be a man

Strong and powerful truth be told I'm weaken submitting spontaneously extending me dedication and devotion. My agreement blindingly to only please myself I'm in love selfishly.

To chat without worry of undivided attention while noting observation of your movements.

The pain of beauty weighing its limits against the dominion of our relationship sacrificing all that has been proven to be demanding. Tunnels existing useless crawl spaces beneath beds.

Most often times cry of wanting what I already have suffering of love now provoked dwelling in undesirable places, comfortable mythological response in reality.

Take my love, centuries from now one will understand what it Was that I left behind in its balled-up grief Wrinkles of tears trapped In lines of illustrating life.

Romantically invaded by love songs the oceans make leaves from tress backup singing

Birds with nice hooks sitting thinking Candlestick sit upon tables burning while we press our feet in the sand. My hands in your hair whispering in your ear. I live for simplicity in moments those glorious smiles you make. Mated souls sitting vertically in the corners looking upon the umbrellas near the fire place aside from the angels that sat on the mantles looking down. Rays of sunlight shined through clouded stained-glass windows. Rays of light so heavenly golden majestic particles extracting the beautiful essence rousing all godly struggles.

Gazed and still reciting the oaths of prayer. Sitting there imitating perfections of our soul watchers representing the faithful leading the humble through all directions of life.

I didn't think to grab my umbrella it links me to wet roses passed from my hands to yours while we sit and watch the sunset over the lake walking back to our lodge we step over puddles that reminds me we'll take many steps towards the right direction. It was the sound of running water that repeatedly invaded my judgements to stroke your body head to toe while engaging in a conversation from the side of the bathtub. The fragrance of your hair filled the room from this wet rainy day imagining the sweat running between your breast while the moisture of my fingertips connected to your clitoris those slow releases walking towards the warm soak running just to find love. Hands tucked beneath your hair eyes illuminating different smiles. I Remember my last glance at the mirror seeing pieces of whom I was finally saying goodbye to it's over stay welcome Unrested and broken inconsolable provoked by an unavoidable rant of foolishness.

Pride had no way of being responsible. At the close of the door time rested inside that mirror pointing 7 and 3 it was only seconds I hurt of stabbingmemories before turning around facing my love waiting before getting ready to

knock unsure about what was in store. Immediately words rapidly. I'm over whelm by my actions these are unsweetened afflictions that leaves my converses filled with distasteful charm of non-reasoning. Its unfortunately I've lost moments I could have passionately kissed and held you instead your absences comprised my intentions.

I've nothing but unsettling desires pleasurable to grant you with the particulars I find engagingly inflamed me of your common beauty. Submit onto me what you've never taken account to giving even yourself. And he froze looking upon blushed cheeks Widen eyes awaited his words to release her. Behind those stone walls rain fell swiftly beading off the center of the umbrella each tracing the trails of the last trickling down beneath where soft hands gripping Uneven breathes of panting helplessly gasping with the fluttering of their hearts. Tingling of wondering eyes aggravated by the thoughts of the forbidden Circumstances Illrepressibly even in beautiful things unrelated I find a way to place you in scenes.

It's handles wooden stain perfectly curved art designs it's resonated charm hand crafted marvel of stained beauty Under its

Blissful joy. Chasing rainbows distinguishing flaws hidden in the mist of emotions running from the adolescents of growth Parting cries and screamssitting near riverbed writing in the tears on my window looking upon the painted skies Lost behind burning candles 12 umbrellas compilation destined to last out eternity. A quivering moment professing love dreaming imagining a life before mine.

Footsteps echoes haunting hallways. Tick tock admiring the way my soul Climbing placing you on my pedestal awaking the aroused beast it's just another ordinary day with these presentations of images in my mind pieces of separated unexpectedly.

The smell, the floor, his shadow Images mirror us in his shoes Woven socks reminded of lamb a sign of god's blessing Pants anchors. A universe beneath the belt she had fallen off the earth indicted to the savory nature refer you as happiness was denied her own existence. Erosion and eclipses

Tidal Wave Victory was hers endless Vanishing desires chosen to expose you thenecessity of privileged admiration. Vines grown from the brinks of seed exchanged atoms and matter united a strength rising up of love.

Unimaginable tenderness provided. While people search for more responsible lovers and have great mates.

You can love someone without anything to wear and feel fully clothed. Can't you tell body to body the heat that keeps you warm. I watch people pick mates because they make perfect presence for everyone else. In the shadows suffering from the monstrous effects. A beautiful beast untamed out of control nothing to offer but harmful words. Love isn't how one may be seen but how they open you up to be different, finding pieces to yourself that you may have not known.

Most selfishly think maybe a laugh or 2 helps but its injury to insult. How dare you when you've been considered everything. So be it I'll be your nothing.

Nothing shall I find to lift you.

Nothing shall be provided.

Nothing shall be missed

Nothing will bring life to what has died in your selfish ways that provided nothing close to love. How dare you pretend love wasting emotional ties, these could have been laced and buried in a heart that would have shed, tears to taste. "Just a drip of love", chocolate flavors melting over sweaty labors.

Distinguish from others carrying the load on their back. Interrupted and paused you adding more weight pressing harder waving in the air at friends. Yielding to hear only groans ... Broken back but you beat & beat them more.

I've accepted the betrayed emotions denied passionate verses of spoken words.

What haven't been said by thy mouth attending to small particulars that naturally aspired me to love.

The beauty that I found in your smile began ambitious means to suggest speaking at lengths. My desires to be healthy equally in converses this was to farther the exchange of common friendship. I'd share a lifetime of blindness shall you have all happiness in regards to what would I give.

I'd never see any sparkle but feel the grace of love attacking me. In short, I imagine myself disarmed and rescued from suffering extremities wishing.

You'll never know the cruelty of me passionately pulling away crying over vented confessions. Should your name never be called without love. I paint objectively how we should speak to each other yet I'm unsure if those would be your words. My only envy is others smiling when we are now.

I remember sitting idle while others converse we had nothing charitable of giving each other.

I'm a man cloning a life of love Erasing his shadows the place where the truth foldsand responds as my enemy in the minds of the intercepting. I've cloned salvation left out the cold with its battered pieces Let scattered in wood sparkling as valuable jewels expected to be magical.

Hidden in the favor of its enemies lying to the creation of ideas intentions

Perfectly predestine to concentrate ill fortune for those whose to identify with the truth.

They didn't say who, when, or what but it's not a secret. I can bet you that its dying to come out.

They didn't say who, when, or what but it's not a secret. You'll always hear you must know someone to get somewhere old saying cloned to feel voids. The wrong understanding of life the life of one that's been cloned. It will remainbeing the right one for others to know.

Condition your mind to accept things you're not use to the choices are always yours. No need holding on to things that we don't want in our lives. No one is holding you to rules only the outward thought in which we're perceived do we make matters important.

Life is only once lived with the things you want sacrificing to be seen as 3. Learn yourself will bring about change in the possibilities of growth Most only know how to live one way. If you can't see it y even question another's ability in the mist of it all Everyone so busy trying to portray roles instead of becoming who you are in a brighter light. I'm a man cloning.

The stem talking to the petals grow with me Share your secrets. Wrap your arms around me I can feel your moisture the condensation of changes evaporating.

Love and its warmth, leaving others out in the cold wondering what it feels like.

Lost looking for anything that resemble a feeling that can't be performed.

While I hold you through the toughest storms Petals and I shall protect & cover you until we are uprooted together I reserve my love my faith my spiritual being to understand the selfless devotion to serve. The deeper I get the less places I must hide. The darkness within this hole shines light from the inside.

Only to feel the clarity of my thoughts I climb & climb.

Don't look down I tell myself its only darkness beneath me but the light shines on me.

Silent disturbance sorting colors Silver skies romantically holding clouds

Parting with tears a poet known as Prince reference to as Purple rain.

Permanently stained canvass drowning in different orals striking everyone who

Witnesses Its clashes of joy sorrows and pain. I get to define each of its meaning.

Eyes closed are yellows upon brown Red parts lip that lustrously seek Figures mounted sweating in dark thrusting towards the magical moments of ecstasy. These passionate desires exploding insulting the shameful personalities forgotten to be human. Everything of life form lives in purpose uprooting as vines supporting us, the cattle of the earth. Aren't we ants next to trees, giants in only our world". "The irony in everything seen and touched. Letter's read protect mother earth after sucked of life for oxygen. These pages painted upon painted life without substance. Now I lay murdered by hands that cut and grinded me but couldn't kill my beauty. Eyes seek my texture to feel, even after stripped of my bark and leaves shaken. Imaging beast unseen someone will dress me. In paint imitating, what has been discovered I've an energy undeniable in beauty.

Private Thoughts The Unrehearsed Verses

My serenity has bitter sweet moments.

Expressions of anger takes control of me.

I am a product of my father's lies.

I am he that cries, he that hungers to feel good when reminded you got your father's eyes.

I am he that deny the truth about things people say to me. Only to except your father's a good man.

I am now a man shaping a father to be my son.

Show him to love and trust just as the day I was born.

He often stayed out late. I stayed up late nights hoping tomorrow was just a mistake.

You'll be here and wrap your arms around me again.

Even though I own the vision he never seen, A father boasting for the body of a son.

While this time wishing my mother was bloating.

I carried my first image from her womb never heard his voice wouldn't even feed me semen.

I was the pacified child secretly in my mother's arms.

She often whispered, you'll inherit wisdom use it to inspire others, help them too, from hurt and pain.

I was just the first-born son the second reason to alibi his freedom

The third voice that cast reasons to point out another man not to trust.

The forth right thing he'd done so wrong, In the mist of it all, I was, I am and always will be the secret kept from his other women. Disunity has a price.

He found excitement in the one he said to love. He humored himself with hugs and the way she twerked her butt. She gave all she had to offer alone with pride and dignity.

He proved his love with his animalistic aggression spilling what came next over her face, she couldn't hide her broken will, exhausted, through meditation.

Lost in what they believed, seeking what we sow, enduring the pain from what once was known as pleasure building walls around peace.

Abandoned of all energy just to find truth again. She breaks her silence. Is this all I am, what do you see in me. A lost soul mother never told the stories of her life before she found serenity again.

He justified loving her with his wallet old bills stolen from his family.

New shoes waited, heat was a day away from the account being closed. She said thank you, but he had sowed a seed and she wanted him to rest in realizing she was another that got the pleasure of resting her head on his chest.

Sweet serenity the satisfaction of lust aggressive rotation of thought.

Yes, then no exhaustion of love, your arousal, nails in my skin, anxiousness, heels hard-pressed in my back watching my body descend over yours to enter your rhapsodies.

Tongues flicker across your breast, the wet exchange of satisfaction, on hands and knees, mouths open expecting to reach climax.

Trapped in silence can't articulate what she means to me. Alone with my thoughts I'm only half the man to utilize circumstances to acquire love from the depths of our souls.

For the most part separating ourselves from what has been passed down dared to overcome.

My poem erupts the ignorance in truth

Why mothers and fathers lie with intimate insecurities.

Engaging in conversations Seeking meaningless vows of love.

Nights past lying in bed giving the loyalty of their energy to someone else.

Therefore, it would cause one to question resentment within one's self yelling out "who am I?"

I call myself by name but mix the two.

I recognize who to talk to but mixing conversations wanting the one body to be the soul that consoles serenity.

I am the Mother and the father suspended in the reality of a deaf child blind to the disillusion.

Lines of communication broken with men, we shadow the truth often never uncovers the scars and bruises left in the mind of youths. Now women stuck in relationships afraid to be open to experience the blessings of her king.

I must resume the responsibility of my thoughts after they arrive in the minds most often results in miscalculation of judgments.

To remember it's to concern with a mind and heart to understand life and social disadvantage people.

In every situation we face, or make judgment on may not always be the best position for the people we do it to.

This isn't to say the right decision hasn't been made its only to inform you that this may be far different from any case thus far. On the corners of the dresser sits 2 glass frames celebrating reasonable devotions.

Everything I've concerned myself with in every prayer, praises where plentiful to my logic.

These things lead me to skillfully demonstrating what love is.

The profound new beginnings in languages unfamiliar to our opportunity to understanding.

A satisfied discourse continuing choosing beautiful feelings of safety to rest divine affection.

Love exposes the sweet of kisses aspiring to express the suppressed intriguing curiosity.

When I look closer the imagined perplexed self-pity of need a desire insisting to taste, touch, feel, and request all that one must give.

The endless thoughts that connects us happens to be the lost energy that consumes me.

My every reason I pick and choose with every thought often time sharing different parts of me with other connections.

Love is the release of my joy the divinity of light the beginning of everything.

You're the apple to my temptation, first sin done wrong in which I found everything right. My last rib broken within these things I find reason to offer entities lusting for pieces of the truth that leads me running back to ends with no clue. Love is seeking a future that opens you.

Dying in the darkness with my pen bleeding ink unknown of what Will come of the next line certainly in the twilight of the mind. Rambling for simplicity the softest thoughts holding on to disputes of humanity. Dwelling on lies with no truth in trying to trust transforming love from mischief learning what I had not known of rating myself.

I had all but forgotten those unaware rigged tears of violence, taking stock of my valuable in my weakness.

My pen bleeds without restraints. Here I sit mourning, wondering no explanation a vanish artist thrusting words upon old tree's chopped of living just to hold my tears to think I didn't shed a tear for it. My life work purpose rest.

I'm a man cloning a life of love erasing his shadows the place where the truth Folds and responds as my enemy in the minds of the intercepting.

I've cloned salvation left out the cold with its battered pieces

Let scattered in wood sparkling as valuable jewels expected to be magical.

Hidden in the favor of its enemies

Lying to the creation of ideas intentions

Perfectly predestine to concentrate ill fortune for those whose to identify with the truth.

They didn't say who when or what but it's not a secret.

I can bet you that its dying to come out.

They didn't say what, who or when but it's not a secret.

You'll always hear "you must know someone to get somewhere" old saying cloned to feel voids. (You must go somewhere to meet someone) well as someone must meet you somewhere where both of you are wanting to be.

The wrong understanding of life the life of one that's been cloned.

It will remain being the right one for others to know.

Condition your mind to accept things you're not use to the choices are always yours

No need holding on to things that we don't want in our lives.

No one is holding you to rules only the outward thought in which we're perceived do we make matters important.

Life is only once lived with the things you want sacrificing to be seen as 3. Learn yourself will bring about change in the possibilities of growth. Most only know how to live one way. If you can't see it why even question another's ability

In the mist of it all. Everyone so busy trying to portray roles instead of becoming who you are in a brighter light I'm a man cloning. The stem talking to the petals grow with me, share your secrets, wrap your arms around me. I can feel your moisture the condensation of changes evaporating love and its warmth, leaving others out in the cold wondering what it feels like looking for anything that resemble a feeling that can't be performed. While I hold you through the toughest storms.

Make a fool of me I can't endure the usual words strange ideas accompanying old feelings.

Love my youth rest the lids of your eyes over troubled muscles within the folds of tracks near my waist.

Pause the sounds concealed beneath my voice carelessly whispering the jingles of take me now.

The confused observation of my heart leaps hurrying away from influenced opportunities to advise love.

I only hope to be a fool, laugh at me, exploit the possibility anything you can use long as you use me to...

The lining of her garments calmed my lack of self-control. The suitable responsibility of finding ecstasy.

A precise securement to arrange your body next to me. Lasting quality of intimacy.

What are those gifts I crave and lust for?

The charm and harmony of your ratchet soul has made a darling in the swiftness of my heart.

Groves of roses hold glimpses feared of losing & blessing gentle preservation of future bliss.

The bitterness of this thing is blind to possibilities. Bring to end formation of invaluable doubt.

The splendor of radiant beauty chases what I want most. Seeking external use of what I may find to be good lustrous serenity.

Why should I not reveal the concealed power of your fertility. Consider what has consumed my tiring thoughts.

I can't do to myself what I want to share. Each shred of dignity should be ripped away. I only desire an opportunity to expand my significant.

How confined should we be to penetrate deliverable sweet orgasmic oceans.

Strides to capture the winds of breathes. To dock lips near the end of passages to pleasure.

I admit I cannot satisfy my thirst of your salty water.

Nor shall I restrain arms or legs leaving you to chase your soul....

"I'm convinced for now, flamed ash to not be touched let it burn.

Love is incompatible inconsistent to when and where I began to feel.

Can you account for that moment without words spoken?

Was your heart engaged at the exchange of words. Thus, this wouldn't support my heart when I set eyes upon you.

Naturally I'm confused had I began to be fair to myself or should I feel cheated.

A foolish heart had perceived love existence yet it wasn't a valid exploration for my feelings.

A contradiction that stood alone.

Why should I believe what I remember if it's different from time?

My imagination has been extended to dwell at length. Here I sit remain trying to provoke a revival of feelings.

What constitutes a primitive affair without mixing where you or I loved one another.

Certainly, hearts go through emotional emptiness how would we distinguish if there was anything to offer.

The remains are opinions we introduced to restore time in between to be investigated.

I chose to find the part of you I didn't know.

In my search, we were already connected. There you were holding my fibers within your fingers ready to pull me closer.

"I'm now a mere understanding of what you recognize as pieces. "You've clothed my will!

Unmistakably baring warmth to a soul that only makes happiness greater than the reality.

"I'm eloquently desiring " the softness of your skin. The secret of a comfortable beginning

Let it dress my nakedness. Bring your phenomenal tools to tighten up drippings.

Study my chemistry, master breaking up my elements.

Find the basics for our existence, in shared space educate me on loving you. I'm to drown within this body, without you holding on to me. Help me breathe! Resuscitate me! I feel myself slipping away.

The condensation of agony depriving pores from waters that dripped of eyelashes.

Fragments lay ahead I've already repaired functionally out dated.

Should my hands not vine umbrellas? Shelter my love during storms displaying discomfort.

Shouldn't hired hands be equipped? Unfolding allegiance to long legs growing lustrous skin.

Abandoned conversational sunsets packed away disowned & left to swim the oceans of memories.

An atlas of stars aligns the sky some running to find our wishes we whisked away.

My knee hurt of holding my hands out front of me, engaging your depth rejecting eternity...

I sleep with my books they tell every way I'm arranged each reason to feel.

Looking at them turns me into a different animal the way I scribble hiding words kissing them in corners.

Allowing them to be wild as they can, stretching the hands of many lover's as they can touch.

I watch as they arouse ecstasy. So much guilty pleasure I'm drawn to make love threw my pen. Locked up behind black lines blue & white jump suits.

To see me chase what turned on the gloss that's erased from lips fast as it goes on.

Eyeshadow smeared behind a smirking smile. Lashes blinking while talks about to the curve of its tips.

"Ink do your thing "taking off high end clothing of the boogie.

Look at her with her hands on her hips. With that cute nose & designer frames.

Different patterns of leopard prints clawed from different animal. Dictionary defines her every move before She gave herself to me.

Yes, he told me about your breed. No appreciation for passion influences love living illustrating emotions of lyrics and all intoxicated ecstasy, awareness sensations ....

Too early in the morning for this. My pen is more than a long hollow shaft releasing the ultimate orgasms...

Next to them my headphones playing loud music from the overflow of being turned on...

Good morning world.

Chocolate Woman

Chocolate woman, Cold and needing to be warm by my touch. God created your perfectly Curved body stimulating my mind without light skin.

Chocolate woman, I've laid and craved you for hours Touching myself thinking of nothing else. Unwrapping your cover needing a taste. I'm a chocolate fan. With an appetite for you.

Chocolate woman, see it's just Miserable me with an addiction to sweets the taste emancipates me. Juices of your taste Stays with my teeth and tongue the root to my mouth covered your delicate treats.

Chocolate woman, my heart races love in every beat. Fingers slithering you open to keep you to myself enjoying a chocolate frenzy. Wisk me away bless my eyes with precisely What you think I can't stand, kisses in little drops.

Chocolate woman, I'll label you Hershey. General warning, ice cream in your secret place, milk chocolate vanilla taste mixing flavors. You never seen what can happen to you while I eat ice cream.

Chocolate woman, see me with your eyes feel me with your tongue. How many licks does it take to get My favorite shake, (rotation) Up and down. Stirring it around and round. I wish I could savor drips of you.

Chocolate woman, I didn't want nobody but you. Your voice imbalance my position to be alone without seeing you, touching you, and feeling these crazy desires. Seeing you allows me to know that somewhere we missed out on the purpose of what living really was.

Even though we live separate lives our hearts connect when we are close omitting the fact we also deny what we feel.

I get so bored doing what people assume to be normal.

Maybe I'm on a journey and you're not here.

Who else listen to words that only matters to you. Besides nothing's wrong with loving you.

Endure strange feelings. Youthful eyes gaze upon each muscle near my waist, concealed you will find someone new within my voice those tones of desperation wanting to observe the burning of those flames we once whispered. Take these opportunities take my advice, take me and all I have to give.

Would it be in between that we've invented to imagine our best? Similarly, to my past, flames burn no reason why you should believe ashes haven't heat or flames not exist.

Love is incompatible inconsistent to when and where I began to feel. Can you account for that moment without words spoken? Was your heart engaged at the exchange of words. Thus, this wouldn't support my heart when I set eyes upon you.

Naturally I'm confused had I began to be fair to myself or should I feel cheated.

A foolish heart had perceived love existence yet it wasn't a valid exploration for my feelings.

A contradiction that stood alone. Why should I believe what I remember if it's different from time?

My imagination has been extended to dwell at length. Here I sit remain trying to provoke a revival of feelings.

Question

Life, love, happiness, pain

I've timed my death it's a long way between who I am and the memory I leave.

Footsteps erased sound of the voice that made mistakes no longer punishing the ears of lover's.

The loss of summer kisses running in the rain.

The breeze of love that supplies relationships a new start of something fresh rides no one lies.

Life unfinished timed by rules questions, priorities, morally, advanced, ethically.

Translation increasing the desire to give love with no boundaries.

Love in a way nothing seems to replace the one everyone knew.

I can melt my favorite desserts with 3 words unused.

My chocolate drop shape and hold me don't be confused.

I love nice things to hang on to, nice words each are only verbs overlooking you would be a foolish excuse.

Not just living to stay till the end I find myself living to find that place we began...

Favor me with your words let me see what it is you miss.

I'm laying here thinking of your touch.

Hands at my face connecting minds.

Plugged, charged up ready to taste neck bites gasping thinking dam what's next.

Fingertips playing instruments of skin fine tone to play a chocolate master piece.

You climb on my shaft, drop down a half note and quaver. A minor key stroke up to a half a beat creating bass banging everything in the opening.

Eyes locked to the beat, nutting continuously from a crochet holding onto minimum trebled trembling reaction. Taking control as we swing freely against trees behind rocks.

Crawling on river beds double chocolate so sweet. Fuck me before you drip on me. €€€£££££€€

Never knew myself until someone told me how they thought I should be.

I couldn't live until a part of me died. Suffered complications of acknowledgmentswithout feelings of success.

Spirit lost and wondering doing what everyone else do walk awhile then fall off.

Claim the love of my maker when I didn't trust my feelings biblical terms or didn't know him at all.

Chased empty thoughts of verses that was repeated

Thy shall thou shall not.

Learned words without cleansing my soul.

Gave away my depths to keep the parts of people that wasn't any good to me.

Listen to what they needed to keep me.

The wise lives alone trust only what he sees, nothing about what he believes.

Truth doesn't belong to his imagination.

The lost was forgotten

Past left to reform futures.

I haven't properly introduced myself I am trapped in feelings holding onto your hopes of love lending your strength desires that haven't been inhabited.

I'm cringed sensible in a bed unaccompanied by needs unsure what I was looking at until I saw shoes underneath the laced panties.

Purple satin arousing. I thought, now I'm drowning sensations crippling control over my hands as they search for a suspected lover.

Eyes ex-ray walls where pictures promised ecstasy.

My ears replayed your intentions the beautiful life stories you previously mentioned.

I listened to crying hearts so filled with love ambitiously hunted each other.

Chased thoughts of me and you in these sheets until you placed your body with in my view.

Here is where it all began your lipstick wrote the perfect notes against my skin.

Love me tonight, tease me from my nipples to my wet pink lips.

Taste the best of me, erase what's left of this burning flame torturing the center cavity of my soul.

I all but imagined being the clouds forecasting 90% chances of showers of pouring rain.

Thunder storms increasing hungering touches igniting lighting.

Screams out loud quaking feet to neck.

Fearing a world existing with no control feeling pieces of you recreating a climate needed for your existence.

A place where love's only meaning is a kiss.

If only caressing was caring and sharing was burying shattered pieces that people hide from us.

Escaping negativity was ecstasy positively granting you passionate feelings 3rd degree.

Everyone could see love inside us

Trust with a scale

Anthony Green

Lust was marriage

Epiphanies undressed you

Roses orchestrated perfect moments sounding off symphonies

Loves only condition was being with you

Words undefined in relationships

Perfection was aged was beauty

Death birth religion

Trouble invent new ideas

Seasons restored feelings again.

Had it been me I'd love looting loud lusting languages lasting longer licking like love left leaving you screaming for your fix.

Chocolate Carmel accessing declinations of flash backs standing in glass slippers.

Dusty purple shaded eyes, melon sweet lips deliciously displayed.

All the substance I'd bottle & keep hidden for my own personal use.

All of you melt within absent touches of me

Diagnose this temperature you've given me shakes shivers and thrills.

Ask what sedates these ill tendencies that react to verbal ascent with visual insight to what I've yet to seduce.

Carmel displayed as a delicacy, drip a taste on my tongue!

Just a taste of your neck, bone between your thighs, legs dripping sweets all over me.

Tease the thought even if you can't understand what you're doing to me.

Grapple hands on his chest

Her head beneath water swimming in a drift catching breaking branches that wouldn't support her weight.

Finally, she was sure about being on solid ground ready to allow his seeds to be planted.

The taste of salted tears watered her growth.

The identity of who she was never seen until conversations took place on the shores of his shoulders.

A treasure never haunted or dug for. Igniting a fever for a rare jewels polished reflecting only her face as keeper.

Garments laced ready to be unveiled in the spring that followed.

All it took was the passwords written in his look, no words could remind him of broken pieces she tried to replace.

He had become a pirate stealing all she had left throwing his people overboard just to have her to himself.

Now she'd be his prize her seeing him as treasure. One becomes hostage the other would carry.

Faded memories shedding light

Different situations to stop love just to return reasons why I loved

Anthony Green

Who where you

You never knew love

Never knew hope

Didn't find desire

Still don't know you

Unfortunately, accomplish Is something overlooked

Loyalty is mistaken

Brussels of brushes paint pictures of love I can't explain.

Dripping across pages.

Hearts mistaken just lost pedals underneath the brush

A hungry me needed a satisfied you.

Now looking

I painted

You were missing

My introduction to you became thirst of my desire lost inside changes, but comfortable inside me loving what can't be held inside me.

I release what nails you and me.

I painted what I wanted us to be

You lost the desire to see.

All that's left is pain and misery.

She cried awake lost separated from her identity.

Refused to fight for something that wasn't in her grasp.

Divided by people who claimed they knew her yet unfamiliar with her identity.

Captured and erased by what they wanted her to be.

Purposely chased everything but what she needed

Sweeping away the broken pieces shattered within her

Empty people sitting on shelves taking up spaces.

Touching or speaking cracks causing breaks in them.

Afraid to open the door to the other rooms,

When the wind blew you'd hear a tone each one squaring, it's her making the noise.

Tops off those fragile bottles she dusts them off carefully placing them back where they need to be.

Each watch her leak with the holes draining out of her unique openings. She was the masters of all glasses

the only one without a label.

Hers was peeled and torn.

Raggedy edges to match her heart.

A victim of love.

A victim through circumstances outside loving, peacefully, & smooth.

A victim inside scraped torn battered and bruised.

A victim hit and stabbed on sight. Experiences of rejection wanting attention to make laughs while sacrificing personal positions.

A victim without bandages stitched trying to work it out being handy. On medication, a drunken high hearing cries.

A victim letting go, giving up lost and finding truth.

It starts here with you.

No longer feel the need for a life linked to my feelings.

It isn't necessary to collect particles lost in your soul. Some mysterious, & others are different takes on life.

Yet everything stays the same no morning coffee.

Dark lover, honey brown morning sweet.

The steam calms my head when I began to think of sips.

The taste of" you on me sweet escape "placing my fingers against my lips. Erase do this again!

Placing my fingers against my face, warmth consumes exhilarating pleasures. Drip drop, creams into your coffee.

Just a thought gets me there, that says a lot.

Comforting thoughts of loneliness in this room.

No mention of love just Rembrandt memories torn & shredded across unspoken canopies.

Such wonderful things you say, but you see me I'm free no dependency trapped in another's feelings taking what may be dished out. No love from me hard sips of your coffee remaining free you can't sell me what you tell yourself.

Sitting alone in a lonely place wondering where's the rest of me.

Lover of this life. My heart hunger for courage to inspire my dignity.

A chuckle from inside morally erasing all I aim to be.

Life and loving
Souls of lovers speaking
to an unrest me.

Anthony Green

Each giving reasons to see
the love placed against my sanity.
Each going in different
So many take parts of me.

Most giving looks of pleasure
others angry at me.

Lovers of life
So many souls pledging allegiance to
Love what they see
Hand after hand all over me

Lips bite and taste every inch of me
How many people are suffers of shivery
Lovers of life.

We run to escape the pain
That we shelter
We laugh to get away
Can't expect it to stop
Life at a standstill
Looking at some part
of us remembering

Perfectly lips traced in red
conforming outlined beauty
Erased is the mentality
that hides within eye lashes.
Mysteriously imagining possibilities between love and attitudes
locked away in you

I can feel you exhale
I see your breath taking
place beneath my

Eyes closed as if it's just a dream
me into you wanting to feel
you move after my thrust

Leopard patterns racing
threw my head I'm a predator
chasing follicles blowing in the wind.
Previewing my hands grabbing
your waist biting your flesh
A sacrifice of my animalistic
behavior my primary condition.

Soul lost with only this voice to carry me
Hung by my feet
Twists and tide
Roped to the top of a stair case
Screaming out to anyone who remembers me.

I recollect these stairs I climbed
Only this time I lost my identity
Friends I've lost far and few
Cherished moments we've had
Laughter over stupid shit
Realizing I
Lost what never belong to me
A friendship out of season.

Dangling upside down I see my feet
Thinking of all the miles they've carried me watching life pass me by while the
Thoughts take me back to the breeze flowing through the trees.
All the beautiful things I may leave behind.
Watching tv with my love smiling at me
Chasing many things that meant nothing
I've all but forgot.

Anthony Green

Running away from the rain
I'd give anything to have
Those simple things again

Rain to run down my face
To feel the freedom of my head
falling back to the sky.
Embracing that taste of the tears of my cry evaporate
Just to have one knee planted on the ground asking forgiveness of my
sins as prayers go up singing amazing grace.

Listening as rain dropping on
Wooden floors humming the beat with me
Wind blowing moving doors pails refilled sitting in the same place.
Angels visit listening crying without me
I have hopes of you all flying with me across high mountains, & rough seas.

My soul is lost do you remember me
I'm the one stood and looked when I was a shame, men exercise a
mockery.
Pointing whispering who knows what they see.

I'm was divided from who I was to what made me see things differently.
If no one else the lord remembers that man I use to be.
Whipped in this life no screams just ambition to fight. Today will me
the power to untie these ropes I'm choking on my own blood lashes of
my own whip.

Roses and flowers seemed to be only a
Unclear view threw dirty windows chalk and broken, smeared I love you.
Nailed shut without hopes of ever being open
Just like seeing things that remain life to never be the same again. There
maynever be another face pressed against the glass.
Life is once and it was all I had
All things considered I remain upside down stripped.

Petals silhouette waters overflowing trust arranged moments.
Flickering shadows take shape in my mind.
Wet bodies dried in flames
Chasing your thought to extinguish the burden of raptures.

Listening for the sounds of pain inviting pleasure to witness your wall
fall relocating to your final inherited ecstasy.
Tell me
What is it you can't say.

Blinded grabbing object appear to be real yet
False as the reality of the sorrow of the one guides me.
The clinched fist held back
Middle finger pointed up.
Hatred beneath the breath
Absolute holding of hands praying with you.
A blind mam praying to never see what's done to me.
Believe it's in agreement the sound of your prayers whispering to
never see.
Lost of time tick tick tick.
Antique cherry clock understands loyalty better than you invested in me.

I'm supposed to be a half a man I still feel unsure of possibilities no
connectionsoutside being target practice for your words aimed at me.

I supposed to prepare I'll pretend I can feel it see what it is your doing
to supposedly help this blind man within me.

I was feed food of glass shaving cutting my tongue reacting only to
impulse keeping quiet hoping not to bleed out.
Standing close by peeping hoping it's the end out me.

Cut tongue and cracked teeth chewing diamonds remain where glass
use to be.
Boiling hatred at the sight of my smiling bling.

Her eyes crave and crawl over me. Her body senses me in her depth. Longing for it to last in her sweet memories.

Her fingertips cut off from touch her mind can't justify what her body feels. Her legs shakes needed to be dangling toes in front of my face.

Starring at windows of time chasing every word replacing with feelings. Lost"
Knowing what to do standing still taking in all the pain love is without questions
Yet questioning everything.

Resulting screams of I'm here for you in reality a lost soul losing, testing your answering

Love

Claiming a collection of feelings, you lack only listing a few words to the ears that hasn't heard the truth within those single vowels.

I and only you listen to these conditions.

Wherever does time go when you become a lie to line up with the alibi in my life.

Screams no longer the silence of my thoughts.

Only the words I can't hear wanting me to feel what you've thoughts of. Eyes glazed wanting to be praised just a little love would turn the key to save a flowered grave.

Love came in threw dirt over my back light came by my eyes.

Moments I knew someone open doors. I, arose to stand still listening to muted sounds. Seeing what you needed to feel.

Bare walls unconstrained by life,

"paint with me what can't be saved".

Images won't last yet we live in an alternate space.

Your stars revolve my moons our not nights accompany conversation that last for days.

Anthony Green

Love awaits me without words to pierce my soul
Without lies hiding behind soft hands and tender touches
Love awaits to hold me to lye next to me revisiting me threw out my
sleep
To be lost in a place where lover swim in rivers beneath two moons
behold what pain the eyes must see taking away parts me.

To embrace life beginning an example as what love needs given what
love does for me without the price of heartache.

If I could find that part of me that knew

Where the sun hides the light inside you that I miss. I'd recover a ray
for myself

Just to see before the morning appears.

You give me peace your glow provides

Salvation in the mist of each exhale I

Lose a little more of you. To think that

Each breath I take with you takes me

Away from you.

My tears are constantly pouring from

My face afraid one day will come the last smile, the last whisper in
your ear

So in every hug I hold a little longer

Every kiss I keep an extra taste

Even in memory I take me out and focus

On you.

Time races against me

I run to see the part of you I've yet to

Meet older, gray yet sweet. My dearest

walk, alone beaches, and unknown

Cities just be

With me hold my hand life isn't long

Enough to cherish what heaven has given

Me to love and teach.

Love I'm listening

Teach me how to understand why

Something so sweet couldn't last forever.

Finally, I understand what it is to

Surrender to words and submit what I feel.

Imagine a universe where souls being the clouds a feeling scream out loud

Fear didn't exist loves only meaning was a kiss

If only caressing was caring, sharing was burying shattered pieces that people hide from us.

Escaping negativity was ecstasy positively granting you passionate feelings 3rd degree.

Everyone could see love inside us trust with a scale

Lust was marriage, epiphanies undressed you, roses orchestrated perfect moments

Sounding off symphonies loves only condition was being with you

Words undefined in relationships perfection was aged beauty

Death birth religion trouble invent new ideas seasons restored feelings again.

Sex is lying next to you to feel multiple orgasms lasting the whole night threw.

Just in case Champaign is the norm keeping the candles lit would cancel storms.

...slowly tracing me with your eyes wanting to see both nipples.
Harden at my lips as they pucker releasing my tongue.
See how my it traces the pattern of your breast.
The harden sensation play with them to wonder what will be next.
Raise your legs I want them in the air let me play with you.
You can expect to release its okay if the bed gets wet.
Lay in my arms while my fingers lay near your clit.
I want to look in your eyes while I do your masturbation.
See what pleasure escapes your lips while your legs lifted and shaking head and body grinding in my bed.
Bite me while I'm lost to ecstasy "you feel that" it's pleasure when you play with me.

Let your legs back down sit up in the bed I only want you wet.

Slide back here next to me I'm still masturbating you I know your sitting on my dick. It's not in you this is my 4-play tool leaning back allowing me tiny bites against your neck while you hit the 15th nut what you expect not for me this is all for you Ahhh shit!

Do you have a clue who's the man in me or the shit I like to do?

My imagination wants what it won't right now, it wants to ignite you.

Just before you get this next one I'll rearrange your clit and my tongue to become one.

Who said I didn't know how to lick a split.

Take the tongue up shit....

round and round then slide down your clitoris

...flick from the bottom to the top causing you to release biting one side of that sweet meat
listening to you moan and squeak.
Watching your arms wiggle right before they dangle and reach.

To panic, say it feels good. Without knowing which way.

gushing out between them luscious legs sexy body lay shaking in them sheets.

Just in case you thought about stopping my representation was made of busting minimum 3

To let you know before I go making love to you like a beast

No ma'am I'm not the one to fall asleep I've 4played you enough to beat it up to round 3 (say thank you)

Would she show me the part of her that I long to see mystical fascinations of shadows creating sex on my wall.

They romanced each other as I watch. I'm I to spy on myself listening to the sounds watching the ups and downs.

I was mostly amazed how you wanted me to be inside you.

The wall shows a different picture you trying to get inside me imagine that.

I found my voice shouting in the wind

It calls to me no scream or whisper

Love

Do you hear me
Drop all that remains unseen use me
Love me for eternity
Love me indefinitely
Love me when no one sees
That love is all I need
A previous love left me
Left me to find the voice
I needed so long
Listening to who I was and now who I become?
A lover of hope
A lover to heal what needs to be embraced.
To taste passion for myself the drips of each drop melts the voice that
remains.
The whispering never shook me the screams never delivered me.
But the shouting echoes in me rippling the drops that melted the voices
left.
Creating that one tear to hide in the rain shouting love like you will
never love again.

Instantly I'm high off what plays out in your head. The orgasmic
pleasures dipping in my thoughts.

Panties alien my thoughts
While you up and down in a robe

Painted nails leaves fossils on my skin. Your toes standing applauding on the floor.
Palms spreaded with you facing south
It's you I have a taste for.

Tell me I'm just a junkie
I find myself fantasizing about the heat between your thighs.
Theoretically if my memory serves me correctly nipples dangled above me as I watch & listening to your eyes echoed.
Tasting can't decide my favorite one joining both each autographing my tongue.
The P.S. read you can have all my fingers dance over me and hands just spank me.
It was then your body woke your hands claimed my head pulled up until our tongues twist. A wonderful sight the music changed.
My head was pushed all I saw was nose, mouth chin. Somehow you ended up om your back where your breast and stomach flew past me.

I found the hive no nectar but it looked sweet so I stop.
I was hard to ignore the rock yet I wanted to taste the honey it was nibbling before your thighs burst open.
The nibble became a delicacy now I got 2 heels on top on me. From over the top of the heels I heard you screaming in need of rescue.
I found myself sliding down one side then the other.
Out pours honey you mimic behaviors of the be. Just when the honey started to flow I put my stick in your honey spot.
My fingers dance with your clit while my stick pound on your honey pot. Its erotic how your displayed Under me love ecstasy 20 toes popping around me.
Laying in shock just a touch to your body gets that to pour out.

I'm not supposed to love
I'm not supposed to trust
I'm not supposed to feel
Yet I find myself loving the feelings I trust in you.

Love listen
Can you hear me
Love stop you got me open
Love hears me open listening to the things I'm not supposed to do.

Finally, I can identify
I can identify why my eyes see the future of someday.
Someday I'll be able to tell you why

I'm impressed by your presence,
learning parts of you that optimistically assails me.
I can feel your impressions
Taking part of me you can't see.

I hear you when you say I can have all of you, would I be right if I took
all of you even the part that I know you shouldn't keep.
All upon your skin I search for any moisture to take in.

I'm loving you but don't trust me
Ill smile in your face
Just to steal a different part of you to keep.
I'm a thief with a habit you're my victim so to speak.
I will shatter your walls you've built to keep lovers out.
Where there was Windows ill come right on in.
The heart for sure I'll take rolled up in your skin to deliver a touch
every now and then.
The impulse from the heart beating inside the skin allows me to take
pleasures no one could erase.
See I'm stealing you If it should be orgasms Ill load them up just to see
you reach another part of you.

No diamonds just the mystery of us the truth of trust. That's the price
of love from me to you. You let me love you from your ankles in my bed
listening at the sound that comes from your gorgeous head.

I've longed to listen well as lingered in my memories of you. Silence of me only hears clues to what we do kissing and caressing you.

Are you capable of understanding me.
I'm incapable of explaining my emotions? Words only express the outer shell, if you take the time to crack it open you will find my heart reaching for you.
Are you willing to reach for me while I'll open you?
The irrelevant details if I can be next to you. A inner applause of feelings clashing at the sight of you disturbing all that I'm familiar with.
Is there such a thing as love
with familiarity.
The smell of you confuses my touch wanting to taste.
The taste of you wants me to devour all your juices.
You're not just sex everything before you were practice for what was real.
Is the real part of you ready for what most cant except (love)?
Your ecstasy without the mist taking pieces of me slowly rearranging my reality. My deepest secret my deepest desire is to be admired by only you. To be the only woman to have a man for her on personal romantic escape, is there such a thing as love the way you understand me.

How long will u love our chemistry how long will my kiss last before I'm your past.

How long is to long you are being without us living to our love song.

How much can you take before your heart breaks if I'm to make mistakes.

How many times will you listen to my promise if most are stolen from wanting to share moments of ecstasy you and me.

How much of my life can I spend with you

To count the Times I make love to you?

Can i count on you to look me in the eyes to remember each time we've embrace each other. See the number of your touches to wonder was it too much or not enough. I stand here looking in the mirror thanking about every time. I've counted the lines on your lips how each one matches mine and where it falls in place to release what we chase. I see you in my eyes incarcerating by my lashes every moment. Shackled and chain me whip me with your love drain me of my emotions to tell the truth of how much I love you. I'm guilty of treason my flesh tells my secrets of what my mind wants. My flesh drives me wonting to openly caress and undress you. To be on display to want others to see the magic we make happen when you're with me. you imagine things that would happen if I'm in you. All the whispers and jealousy to have others desire and want what happens only when you're with me.

Soft white linens stretch from the hills of my shoulders to the arch in your hills.

Looking across this ocean of waves I surrender my curiosity of the ships sailed and boats that never made it. I ask myself where there no captains exploring your depth, while I listen to the stories of voyages shipwrecks and lost and found. While looking across that ocean I found something in you I never knew but I was mesmerized by mirages of sea shells and star fish at the shores. Once again, I want to place my tattooed stars over you change your day to a quiet peaceful night. Only to hear the sounds of the Wales one flapping her tail the other feast. Beautiful display as the moon comes thaw windows shinning on our souls just you and I.

How long is to long
Wait for me
Wait for the part of you that needs me.
My heart is on an express train headed to you. I've waved by to all the things that caused me to cry.
Wait for me I need you
I need you to hold my eyes
And brush my lips. To verify what I mean to you.

How long is to long
Eternity is missing forever and it's never only to never forget I and you
are forever thru out eternity.
I need breath to save till death to awake in the face of my angel to dry
her tears with what's left.
How long before
Your face brings me all of you

I can't wait to speak in front of you lips for your ears to lean forward
to listen.
To look into your eyes to see myself undressed dripping sweat glancing
at your eyes closed dreaming in the reality. Mouth to be open ready to
speak go deep in me. The shakes the shivers the body releasing while
your legs go up and unlock a river. To flow all over the sheets

Slaved
I'm chained until u release me I'm a slave to you. whip me as my soul
cry to you. To run away with u in the night stopping by a stream u on
top of me flipping u fucking you under the moon. Howling near dawn
while the smell of my honey fills the air close to cum. Cum with me
I can feel you dripping on top of me.
I see the bones come out your back and the way your ass react wiggle
gripping snatch only the tip ..Wait...wait I'm in love with the way you
grind in between my hips you say .It's yours how do I make you stay .We
are free feel the warmth of me removing your halo
A cross between sin and what it takes before you break
I'm thinking twins we are free
To love, listen Awww-awww
Shi'i
I'm going back in Ill love u under all conditions
Right now I crave only to be in you
I only want to carry on give it to me listening to u beg for me take me
to another place.
Stimulated by joy and the noise u make slapping that brown
banging as your putting nails in me, go deeper you say.

Tell me what happens!!
That feelings you have when all I have is going while your fingers and
its toes stretch and reach.
Lost teeth imprint left behind on branches near the leaf. Jumping up to
run half dressed in the wind
A chase till the end just to stop to do it all over again.

To sit in someone's eyes with the flame of love burning your thoughts
before you read the pages of their hearts. Braille impression laid upon
skin awaits touch for translation to arouse essence of epiphanies

Thoughts washing the joy that sprints & leaps ridges just to find
themselves in a title wave of fire to be near you.
Surfing threw the flames drilling for submerged water to fight the fire.
Not any water will do only that from a mysterious place.
Wait for me sit on this rock until the water flow through.
Can't confuse t sweat from an upward pour of rain.
Eyes locked lifting the rock as water flows out mysterious place with a
mysterious taste.

I heard you scream when I shouted water coming out.

Words
Desire isn't met until the feelings meet the words everything sounds
so familiar love sounds less than an idea that's imagined. Love isn't
enough you can hear and understand the meaning yet its empty,unless
you listen to the soul it shouts a language no one understands but
emotions .A war can be declared both sides fighting for the same
cause .I'm in the middle playing both sides reporting to move forward
telling myself to get out let feelings and words meet how will they
arrange themselves without me being there .I'm no coach but together
we are a team feelings you stand and guard words don't let them say
what they really mean. Talk to words give them a reason to think
it over. Desire close your eyes to everything that may shine because

Anthony Green

beauty is blind listen to words they will translate before you make a mistake. Imagine feelings without words or desire what would it be to keep looking for something that's never going to appear between the 4 of us emerging known as u and me

No one but you

Normally I don't be scared in the weather but I am a little tonight because I'm not use to this one thing I'm so clear on in my life if anything ever happens to me I always say and would only ask The Lord to allow me to see your face you're the prettiest women I know. Naturally beautiful with a spirit to match it before today I was wondering if or was I willing to fight to hold on because of how we got alone but I'll fight to love all of u until I take my last breath I've never loved any one for this long but I'm willing to love you beyond my years

Lost
Your laughter gives me peace of mind, rescuing me monitoring sentiments of devotion hearing predilection of the past.
I never knew you until this moment all the pain you could've ever cause me was forgiven.
I found myself listening for the hiss beneath your breath.
Inhaling the sweet taste of your words digested into my body nurturing the boiling points that's arisen.
Poised in your presence no control trapped when you become silent aching for your touch.
Memorable moment gazed at curves and soft wet lips, running my tongue across your lips before kissing you.
Remembering to taste the sweetness of your tongue.
Removing the coldness that once lived in you owing to temptation of rapture seeking salvation.
I'm no longer running from my thoughts

I only want to see you after you bust you can say that this was all you
needed.
My needs won't be for filled until
I make love to you over and over
until

I have no urge	< Desire
to call	< Erotic conversation
u friend	< aficionado
I'm fed up	< limp
wanting you	< captured

Only to be thought of before the kiss still I stand here looking at your lips.
Afraid to speak you are perfection the owner of my erection.

Reality
Vast images appear
To the erotic sounds
Of loneliness moans and scream of sexual
Fantasies.
The pleasure of ecstasy coming in the form of poetry.

Reality
The thoughts exist as all hugs and kisses who could ever love like this.

Reality is this
Fuck up, there's no kiss you share with me your as to kiss.
Being separated from love to argue emotions while remaining devoted.

Reality
When the bills due u looking at me I'm looking at you.
Check the bank no funds coming threw we both start holding our heads
on what to do, struggle and fight to get this thing right.
Question every sacrifice before making love at night.

Reality
Who you give your love to after your promises of being true.
Angry faces if your making faces trying to find replacements.

Reality
Love in poetry exemplify things I think of doing to you yet my mind
ignores reality keeps you in my bed rapped in sheets only the visual of
you naked instead, my mouth at the button of your feet kissing upward
to your sweets.

Reality
I see me on top of you grinding for an hour or 2 the thought fades when
I think about that bill that's due.

Reality
I'm satisfied sexually but if I'm going to keep you next to me I got to
give you all of me

Reality
Love is work, work is love, reality is a bitch, the bitch stays on my mind
while I'm on my grind

Mysterious Thoughts

Forever loving in a mystery when I made the decision to break my silence with the greetings that allowed your heart to be attached to the sound of my voice. The mystery of what made the most beautiful smile in you set standards of how I wanted you to feel the intoxicating softness of your lips only to pull away from your smile. With those same lips, I'm lifted with your mysterious words left behind placed together to erase empty spaces. It's no mystery why my will awaits to hold your face in these hands, so many questions without answers slowly eating away at me. Love is slowly the reason why I hold on hoping there's no mystery behind wanting to feel what you tell yourself not to feel. The smiles from old conversations the invading exhilaration of thoughts that leaves you feeling refreshed. We live so close in the same spaces of time undivided by others in our lives connected as if we were the same guided by our feeling satisfied by the thought of touch. Should it be that one should be without the true love the one who has no judgements or no questions about how life is lived and other places are only to care for what remains as a balance between the two. Conversations carries us to mysterious places unknown where time has no jurisdiction the muttered mmm softens the core of me as if you were listening to the sounds of kisses being delivered to your body the untamable excitement of truth releasing tensions of arousal. finding the mist of juices to be the flavor to enhance the rage of ecstasy. My prize is to hold your eyes captive of each performance where there's no mystery. Hold your body accountable for the sensual touches followed by a little roughness. Competing on who loving reveals the most pleasure. Nothing brings me more joy than knowing the part of you that's accepting of every part of me recognizing that this is a gift and I'm open to unwrapping the ribbons of thoughts that are so confusing to others without the sound of voice just exhales of breath should I be without the compassion of how u view and relate to the complexity of vibes and temptations that drives us to escape daily life that brings us to this point. tell me that the tone of my body was never a vision next to your skin and my sweat wasn't what you thirst for over and over threw the night wondering if the feeling you chase ever finds the real thing to be as exhilarating I know opening up can be difficult but I beg of you to take me I'm yours until the next sunrise I'd be willing to make you the delicacy of breakfast in bed to end all sups-ions.

Missing perfection
hums before taking fight to the wind searching for word left behind by her hand.
The My sprits marks spelled love that has spelled me an irrational vindication of truth.
Ruffled feathers falling one lost in the ink tells the story of a revealed secret, to how the magic of enchanted verses exchanged in the elevation of sentiments.
Strolling across paper torn and balled across the floor scathed in my mind.
Missing the image of perfection
A poet lost without a way to elaborate what he sees apart from images without visuals only words to fill in what he thinks.
Relieving motions of hands turning of the door knob as I walk away, from viewing a perfect image of her releasing me after the final kiss.
It was there where I was lost as sounds of laughter fill the room soft tones phones ringing promises of being there soon.
Delighted by prefect time listening to how the day went yours and mind lost track of time.
Now I stand excited you Invested trust and time to say your that perfect image I'm missing.

Nobody gets thirsty
until the water is gone
The taste merely tingling
on tips of taste buds.

Mirages of what once was no longer relevant to reality of old memories.
Excavations of earth you'll never find fossils of my backbone.

I've always looked across the river knowing you where fulfilled an
unlimited supply if it dried.

I controlled the rain
I only wanted to be in the forest waiting.
Watching you plant in the light in the dark your cold and empty of
beauty.

And I shall protect & cover you until we are uprooted together
I reserve my love my faith my spiritual being to understand the selfless
devotion to serve

The deeper I get the less places I have to hide.

The darkness within this hole shines light from the inside.

Only to feel the clarity of my thoughts I climb & climb.

Don't look down I tell myself its only darkness beneath me but the light
shines on me.
My hands travel through lines stopping in places shouting and
questioning my mostintimate desires. If I could tell you how many
hearts I've allowed to invade mythoughts openly leaving me to establish
relationships within myself enjoying it as if there was just the two of
us. I've all but forgotten where its beginning the stimulation of my
pretended reasons to love left me the blame of those broken hearts.
My silence never begged or smile yet it received hopeless romance.

To everyday I give honor to my spiritual invoke experiences to see life through the way love should be given.

Tears should only be seen through reasonable explanations in which we consider to be joyous volunteering laughter to life. My cost to love was split between different pallets of indulgence.

With interests of presumptuous lustful passions and objectively perfections of sex.

Episodes of laying eyes against blessed possessions of hands reached its pentacle in

reality emerging the depths of all my smiles.

Nevertheless, we sit idle longing for what's translated threw impulse desires in which we lack courage to acknowledge verbally. I for better words journal each emotion that I've encountered.

Over time line that I written become the boundaries in which I understand some

human holds no qualities of these experiences besides dreamy observation. I originally started describing life from the root of a log that laid-off my yard as a kid its roots where very interesting that way

What reminds struggles of selfishness of new beginnings common friends become enemies.

No opportunities given to inspire love
I'm a universe alone a virtuous piece of my prefect dream

A conjunction of flesh and spirituality Optimistic qualities.
I'm to distinguish my flaws hidden in the mist of another's emotions

Running from the adolescents of growth.
in the light of darkness listening wondering of emotions

Wanting a smile, I hadn't created surveillance a universe brimming of dangers

Wanting your fear to disabling unsatisfying glances this world filled with life and no love.
Only the seeds of beautiful words defaulted due to an inability to speak them clearly to your death ears.

You're a desirable host in these elements of me subconscious hesitating you furnish the stars glistening in our atmosphere illuminating moving as butterflies mating in our honor
The trees uprooting on grassy hills absorbing my minerals planting an array of flowers.

Waters quenching the thirst of my grounds earthquakes breaking my heart.
The gold that's buried in me shining Iron to be my strength
Diamond's and gems as my feeling sign creators I shall tend to, and love.

Emphasis my duties caress the twilights of my comprehensive perception to receive you being my Queen, never to know pain
Intimacy measured so brilliantly, make yourself want this impulse desire the reason to not want to feel this for nothing else

Sooth endless thoughts that tortures Holding you in silence, Distribute Only
What's submerged get it out your system gives it to nights when you question our purpose of watching others. Pull together the hands that pledge to hold you
Suffer in them equally accompanying this exhibition as apassenger constantly marking

Latitude of our travels. I can't pretend you're not what I want

The mother in what would be my earth.

Had I understood I wouldn't eaten of the fruit produced by our sun.
Look upon our world A sky of water grounds of clouds this effects my

sanity seeing things that's not there. Letting go of what's mistaken for gravity

.... Blow your tornadic winds erupt my volcanos feel my larva run slowly over your seams

Place sand on my beaches build me a house of it with only walls no room still our soils until we

are fertile. Race me to the beginning of evolution, wear Jupiter's ring and I shall drink of your milky way.

Alienate me of my human structure cast spiritual revelations of the tongue to translate our spectrums of resonated particles into beams of light.I wanted to stand amongst the strong but powerless in my own reflections. Replicas in mirrors starring at each other each looking at a different flaw

Quietly

I watch as the fire burning my eyes desire the words written for they could only

view, amazed at the description of the words.

Never did they see the dandy lions blowing with the softness of your breath passing by.

A sententious feeling awaiting inside my nose craving you seeking absorption.

Lip fell into stimulating waters you once bathe in.

All reaching absolute disillusionment of your presence.

The only place I wanted to be was right here laying where I'm lying next to you

Yet I can't sleep because my mind is on you who knew love could be so tuff with you so close to me.

You're dreaming and I'm waiting, only in my dreams we can be as one only you I want to make love

Only me to suffer the price of sleep without

Having the one of my dreams.

Don't cry for me dying every night I cried under the sun the moon steals all that's left

The batted heart that loved everyone the soul that haunted many

The mysterious affairs that left women lonely
Cries uncomfortably displayed as hope without faith.
Don't cry for me my pillow whispers 2 different ideas now change my
mind

replacement of what I wanted with what's next then

Lose control, shower put on your sexy underwear fix a drink pour a
little for me
Pick up your cell phone take snapshots till your turned on.
You got to understand I' m the reason you're in heat.
I want to be there in your flesh since I can't play with it until you're a
mess.
Exhales of warmth beneath your feet your eyes gaze to find mine
A simple succulent taste of your toes hissing musical to tremble your
feet.
The charm of splendid lines wet and glistening.
The desire to feel teeth nudge over nails
Engage to the heart beating in your feet.
Impulses confirmed pleasurable moments similar to those walked upon
sand
leading to waters climaxing oceans.
Securely embraced in my hands I'm intoxicated by your flesh.
The brown of your skin beautiful chocolate drops.
My intentions are to heat and melt the puff and blow until your covered
on the walls.
Soft objections from minor slips of the tongues longing to lay gasping
With hands in the air.
Awkward satisfaction Renewing vitality...
She wanted to be ready tormented by the torched feelings he avoided
giving
The shame of loving a man she was so proud of the magnetic unbroken

lurking of his touch.
Overwhelmingly singling out all she felt.

She wanted to be ready as in her dream.
Although she's wasn't sleep wanting to be awoke

In the very world, she fantasizes about he was all she needed
Yet she was another he wouldn't love & she wasn't ready.
She couldn't except what he wouldn't give.
Exposed to her sound mind, & beauty without definite reason to wife
her yet he lacks love.
Storms of hopeless tears a blush of roses rippled blowing threw her mind

In tornado winds stabbing her heart slathering the pain death of love
She stands in a black dress reading and writing words.
Hanging on to delicate of the words she'd never hear.
You take notice to my notes write to walls that leave you without the
company of me.

Is it strange to proclaim you as my lover?
Is it the same as wanting to exist in the mist of your reality?
Then I remembered you need what's not given seek what you're not
ready for

Everything you know hangs in my life to be a thing of the past.
How can I last with you in my future knowingly life would escape the
point I'm trying to reach?

If I give love without you having a fee.
The price of love is always give up, sometime, somethings.
Essentially what create character to bring u close to me.
I see life in a dream long walks holding hands a woman who loves not
just me but being under the influence of the ring.
Might I wife
Might I love twice
Might I abandon in life
Might I choose to show u what u say u want.
In my mind, you won't to exist but can't deal with my shit.

What it really takes to live
I'm to be the man.
Behind the gates of my reality.
Far from sweet bills and live carefree the price is more than you want to do with me.
I've missed the lines of her body securely tucked away in my memory
Looking from a dream seemingly fix to silence my reality.
The craving for locks of the hair to hang before my eyes drying what once was imagined.

Love sleeping wanting to be awoken by screams, mouths caressing and holding each other apart.

How is it your untouched by my hands and yet I feel as if I'm the one you been waiting for. How is it that we never met and we share a past that connects? What should I expect when we cross paths and you're the greatest of Gods project. I've learn to listen and love through all conditions but you are what's missing see you're the picture in my frame that puts all others to shame. No one is to blame when life changes courses and you began to live again I think that you earned those wings so fly with me no tears of pain just tears of joy and hope to remain focus in this mind frame.

Loneliness
It's not words we proclaim toiling with another's emotional stability I was known to be rescued now. I'm sitting saying farewell to memories. No one order my presence not even you. Yet I remain captive in this extraordinary hold you have over me.
All in my feelings laughing joyously in pain with an oath to love screaming dam you! I'm breathlessly in love with what we once shared. Remembering the last time your eyes love the site of me. The constant replays in my head trying different tactics to touch that feelings tirelessly. I lay hurt and helpless each day with no progress bleeding refusal of words I can't understand. This positive meaning to me trying to fit what no longer exist.

It's impossible to declare trust, fearful of tomorrow my heart has delicate rips. All which came of obligations separating defiance, pausing manners being kind in a just cause situation.

Is it usually how you take what you don't mean and express it upon your face. Maybe it's I that perceive your decisions where linked to an expensive taste of a lady. In truth, I've been the perfect gentlemen Considering everything including what you've never needed.

Quarreling for the same understanding "ridiculous" Playful tools at least pretend, long after we shall be blinded of what should have never taken place. The coldness will find warmth in another Your reflection will stand in another's mirror Fear you've made a mistake.

However, I have to admit my smile will never be upright as it was in our beginning. Sometimes I will be miserable. But I give you up freely, the biggest pain I'm a victim

You can't see me because you love another And I've no one to say love just experiences I admire.

Do you intend to rob me of my lustrous grievances? Once more allow your hands to be cordial with my body. You could win my intention with breath passing my ear I'm at a lost unfavorable to seek your beauty. All in exchange to feel your legs cling to me. I love the illusion but hate my tears because it's not you I'll share love with again.

It's a poor attempt but it's all I have left Prayer is what brought me to this position Now I'm questioning god intentions Yet it's your interest elsewhere that brings us here

Take me anyways

My choice would be to remove all those untrusted experiences making them history. No more thoughts of how's when whys Just except the things I'd do to your mental.

I see beauty indeed I do. "Yes" I see you. Covered sweetness drifting slowly away from me.

For if no reason other than to feel me in your soul I beg of you to never leave. It would be an early death I care not for a burial of pieces of myself I've kept out of harm's way.

I'm at a disadvantage you're without my touch I'm without a place to hold you besides in my heart. Most unusual circumstance I fear to say directly to you, so indirectly. I want to know you threw more than just sight.

Fly with me lift me lay upon my wings Allow my love to Comfort you Yes" love ", it takes charge of me I note every experience I could say more, but why would my foolish feelings intrigue you. Forgive me this is what I say to make lite of this situation. Trust me you'd never worry over a single thing,

Body of love

She knew I was hers in 1000 Memories, of my tongue stroking the bottom of her feet the tinkling smiles departing tender perfect cheeks. Her eyes locked behind bitten lips guarded by the body of my presence fetching sounds Delightful to my soul No one ever communicated explanations of why our exhale pulled us closer. Too bad she's mistaken that I'm to love when I'm hurt in need of that one to void out my pain. Cleverly disguised in touching wanting her to be the one I love. Such a waste of sexual energy Pampering everything but me.

How

The silence of her cries gives me harsh looks. Anger fueled and burn me I can't feel my heart its was lost in the last blaze. Everything in me charcoal and weak but there's a beat of what remains. Vibrations of I love your love holding me listening to my hands dancing with my feet eating me with your eyes. Tasting what you smell seasoning it with sweets how do you give a dam when your watered down. Tossing what you once loved into a position to hate what you can't stand I'm just a man on two feet. My sprits hums before taking fight to the wind searching for words left behind by her hand.

The marks spelled love that has spelled me an irrational vindication of truth.

Ruffled feathers falling one lost in the ink tells the story of a revealed secret, to how the magic of enchanted verses exchanged in the elevation of sentiments.

Strolling across paper torn and balled across the floor scathed in my mind.

Missing the image of perfection

A poet lost without a way to elaborate what he sees apart from images without visuals only words to fill in what he thinks .

Relieving motions of hands turning of the door knob as I walks away,from viewing a perfect image of her releasing me after the final kiss .

It was there where I was lost as sounds of laughter fill the room soft toons phones ringing promises of being there soon .

Delighted by prefect time listening to how the day went yours and mine lost track of time .Now I stand excited you Invested trust and time to say your that perfect image I'm missing.

Pretend you fell in love let's just say we're sent from above would you give up your all in your life without a clue to who your giving your love to .Pretend you never had no other like this lover to open your mind and discover a whole new world nothing like your use to, your lover gave you kisses that other lack as you relax you think back to how your relationship began no one to could relate cause the pleasure of a kiss wasn't all you wanted to do .Thought tumble as your body scream while your insides burn thoughts remind you your just pretending so no need to take your clothes off just get lost in your thoughts. Let's pretend that your mind was now at peace remembering the sparkle of the teeth before the kiss where your lips meet hand to your face can't erase that distinctive taste. Let's pretend it never happen would you do it again if memory could erase would you pretend you didn't like it just to do it again.

Dream

Today I've thought so much about you, more so about us and the ways you laid in my arms listening to me express my thoughts and my fears. It's amazing how your body react to me when I look into your eyes all I see, is the way you want my touch as if my hands on you already isn't enough. Even though it's just a dream, my thoughts of you so are real on down to this note. The sweet smell of you remain softly on me anticipated by your kiss, I await jumbled by your affection to me. When is it do we become all that has been for seen?

Star's

As the night past I think about all the times I let past all the fun things that never seem to last knowing that, I cherish these memories. Breezes take me back into the past of unforgotten laughs under the stars in the night sky twinkle twinkle this night was for you and I. Holding you in my arms thinking and wondering how we began and how this night ends emerging thoughts to find intriguing way I would say goodnight maybe our night began where others stand and wish under the stars in the mist. Here we find what love means unforeseen but our thoughts are among our wildest dreams we shared but one kiss and the magic began to bliss no longer a dream. The stars shine bright just enough to show off the high lights on you face erasing your heart from pain learn to trust and love again. Ask me why on this night my heart started to cry for the softness of your touch it was then I realized I wanted to tell you so much of the sweetest things so let's start with the joy you bring. I offer nothing but for you to continue being my queen to listen and share all the thing that a good life seems. Wish on that star you 'll know how beautiful I think you are, make this wish and love is first on the list. The stars of the night sets just right clouds in the sky still white only thing strange it's night the moon sets half as it's a cartoon but only to remind you of the cow and the spoon.

Rush

A magnet to the soul connecting two spirits, allowing love to rest catering to needs unattended. Running through veins metaphorically speaking, of the same love came with an irresistible urge leaving teeth pressed onto skin. Seizing interest scheming to control the fluctuations of pulse while goose bumps waits beneath the skin. To be an alliance of love seeking to take over the weakest link, to what was the strongest chemistry existing in mental notes. Prowling on hopes of a finales to open new chapters that's fluent with mentioning's of flowers &, holding hands gazing into dreams of love land. Questions relate Is this what it seems what does it mean can it be taken from these dreams if I'm armed only with meaningless things. Are the manifestations of what's chased hidden and erased but better potentials when embraced?

Angel

How is it your untouched by my hands and yet I feel as if I'm the one you been waiting for. How is it that we never met and we share a past that connects .What should I expect when we cross paths and you're the greatest of gods project .I've learn to listen and love through all conditions but you are what's missing see you're the picture in my frame that puts all others to shame .No one is to blame when life changes courses and you began to live again I think that you earned those wings so fly with me no tears of pain just tears of joy and hope to remain focus in this mind frame.

E"s

My heart longs for the idle sound of your voice, this sounds clams it to beat at the right pace. Whispers running through my head, trying to figure out the right words to say. You're in my presents right now I'm not understanding myself, but wanting to say these words. Once more you allow me to inspire you your heart is with in my reach already you've enjoyed my desire to understand and share conversations. My only need is your touch, these hands await you, your body scream for them to moisten the weakest part of you receiving pleasure of just a touch followed by a kiss slowly drafted over your body no parts missed picture this ask yourself...can I handle this

I never knew that the feelings that I'm feeling would be so new they come establish no missing words. Escorted by loves essences evolving to execute old thoughts of what others believe love was. Your love lives in me exercising your erroneousness pushing this strait threw me. Loving you is endless engaged and enforced to energize episodes of epiphanies. To hear you speak of my name is evidence of exhilaration emerging in the way we embrace our emotions. You may have experienced this before without my thoughts or me being the one to expose what you are unwilling to give. Join me in a quiet session there you'll find a room filled only with the soft silent of euphony between the two. Eagered to make this everlasting.

We can't fix the world if we can't fix ourselves

Tears Of Love

Bertha wasn't a woman of domestic qualities although she was a widow whom had taken on the responsibility of her sister's child whom had died giving birth to her first-born Rebecca. She was satisfied with her life although the disappointed of her sister stayed at the forefront of her mind. She never marked out for fortune just a simple life with many values. She ran a cleaner in town that made just enough to make ends meet. Spending the pleasurable parts of her days sitting on the lawn underneath the willow trees relaxing anyway she could. Bertha was a compassionate mother always going out her way to do what needed to be done for the two that depends on her the most. Standing on the porch beating the dust off the carpet calling out Rebecca! Rebecca! Are you ready yet I must get into town before noon what's taking you so long.

It was a day she had awaited Travis prom and birthday followed. Bertha didn't want to leave her cleaners early she still had to make ends meet. The expressions of how proud she was of Travis reached everyone she was in touch with. She was ready to see him in his tucks & meeting whom he had chosen for a date. Although she was needing to be back home before 2:00 she had picked up an extra shift. Rebecca was finally ready they were off to find decorations for the party planned for Travis Birthday. She'd planned a small gathering with few of his friends. Travis on the other hand excited and nervous about asking Rose Fletcher to attend the prom with him.

She was someone he paid close attention to with the deepest sense of admiration. Somewhat satisfied and only shared few of the same sentiments. Rose always showed herself usefully to oblige whatever Travis needed in his studies. In his opinion, she was the best fit for him to ask at least he thought

Travis conversation with Rose landed him a positive outcome for a date it would be the first shared experience with any women of his time. Also learning that she was unavailable for love or any significant belonging to anyone.

Night of the prom they shared intimate conversations followed by nightly walks for days to come. As all relationships, they found mutual grounds for friendship that would last for a lifetime.

It was Travis's Birthday an ordinary day of sunshine even though the weather was ever changing where they lived. Travis was hanging out with friends parting being wild as young people do that time hand come to an end. It was his birthday and wanted to spend time with his family to see what was planned. He had reached the age of 18 granted a lot more freedom than ever before. He was going home by time he reached his driveway checking the mail retrieving paper from the grounds Rebecca's alarms Bertha. Travis is coming Travis is coming! She yelled in a whisper. Oh gosh I forgot to hang banner. The banner displayed Travis name, Becca grab the step ladder hurry, hurry she yelled out

Looking around the room in all sort of directions she spots it in the corner rushing over to grab it. Picking it up hurried to get it near where Bertha was standing. Giving her the end of the banner, hold this as she turns to go up the creaky ladder. She hung one end came back down to hang the other. She had hopes for a striking look on his face. He was as all people love his name personalize to fancy himself a little more. When Bertha hung the other side, she calls Travis! In here my dear. She was as always proud and happy. Rope still align the steps she had left it entangled the hill of her shoe she went flying backward, Rebecca standing looking barely at attention reaching for her once she realized it was going on. Bertha never saw her hand by time it was out for her.

Falling onto the table that centered the floor breaking the glass and knocking everything off it. Travis walked into the room catching a glimpse of the end of her fall mom are you ok. Dashing over to help her back up, Rebecca nearest to her arrived to her aid first. Both now are you ok, Bertha only smile and replied actually I'm not. I'm at disadvantage I love you both with all my heart. Becca and Travis hadn't paid any attention to the surrounding to notice she was bleeding refusly. No stop it was then Rebecca noticed Travis stop, she couldn't get the words out Travis She scream. He turned and look at Rebecca. the words came out it seemed as slow motion now looking to seeing the blood Rebecca's call 911 went unheard. Travis couldn't move. Emotionally locked mind had entered a different state

Bertha recalls giving birth meeting her son for the first time. She touched his face my beautiful baby I love you. never forget what I taught you as her hands fell from his face. Mom! he cried aloud mom! Travis frightened in tears, frantically kneeling before her shaking her hoping she'll awake. Always be fair to yourself he'd remember those words the rest of his life as they replay in his mind. Rebecca what happened both hysterical unknowing what else to do. Paramedics shortly arrives They both pace the floor knowing nothing could be done whimpering throughout the house. Both unsure of the what was next to do. It was a sad occasion most informed grieved as expected. Shock everyone with loss nothing would be the same ever again. After the funeral Nathan Fuller came forth to help as he always had come to the aid out of friendship.

Nathan was a vigorous worker known as honest known to have a few shots most weekends. He was skillfully known and respected by his peers. He and Bertha often traded work for supplies he lived on the other side of the town in a more remote area. Travis invited him to stay awhile until things where stable, he was to teach him to organize the bills well as run the cleaner service.

Drunken nights Nathan would spend the Friday nights at a local bar chatting around with some of the locals. He'd have a few beers to knock the edge off for the week. Unlike most he was a terrible drunk falling over loud and obnoxious. Demeanor changing from the warm friendly guy everyone knew him to be. That was his weekly night life while he had been single and no wife or kids to care for it was within his rights to do as he pleased.

He had followed the same routine for so long without any attention to his person. His needs were unattended in the area of attraction to a woman. He had no feel for one until he came home. Rebecca and Travis were sitting around in the living room watching television. Travis was sleeping with his legs propped up sitting in his mother's favorite chair. It was typical for them to watch space movies reruns on the weekends. Travis, you going to fall out that chair you might want to catch a bed. Yea you might be right, grabbing his bowl and glasses from a meal he'd prepared for them.

Rebecca shouted out to Travis. I knew you wouldn't last, I knew you wouldn't last Mr. all-nighter giggling and teasing him, gone off to bed! Nathan looked towards her oh you won't last while you are bragging over there. Oh, I'm good Rebecca replied. She had gotten use to Nathan coming in with the smell of booze nearly drunken. He was predictable are you wanting your dinner Nathan we put some away for you I'll grab it for you. Rebecca covered in a blanket throwing it back off of her revealing her Indian style position. Stretching her tanned legs to the floor leaping off the sofa Nathan was sitting in the chair where Travis had gotten up from. Seeing her get up he had seen her whole body of releases it was all in slow motion the painted finger nails & mechanical bending and pushing up flexibility of her soften tight skin arms attractive as the jiggle of her breast pull against her shirt. The turn of her head exposed the beauty in her face eyes glowed in a way he'd never seen. She flanged her hair showing off a silent smile. Although it was her normal pose she was often happy and hospitable. More than happy to heat up his dinner Nathan arose up out the chair headed to the dining area not taking his eyes off of her. His disposition was unbeknownst of himself, he tried looking away he began to pace the floor. Rebecca asked is this warm enough for you? Oh yes, yes! just set it there. Can I get you anything else? Well I ugh, ugh yea you can actually. He couldn't help but to think of the outer storage he needed stocking the house with a few meats for the following day. Walk out here with me if you will, he usually done this on Saturday mornings after waking it was one of his many chores. Rebecca was more than reluctant to oblige him oh yea you ready now. Nathan headed to the door and opened it becking his hand for her as most gentlemen would. She walked out the door leaving her shoes behind. Nathan followed looking over her body head to toe. It's nice out tonight she said I often never see the stars but they really are beautiful. He replied, "yes they are, they make me think of so many things." Nathan was cautious of his words gave much consideration to touching her without conduct. He gave his thoughts little actions refusing each with a higher concentration denial. Once at the door they walked in it was dimmed and private setting away from the house. Nathan looked behind him paying attention no one was around. He proposed to her go ahead grab the meats and lay them on top of the table. I'll grab us some bags over here. He was opening the cabinet, it contained bags, tools, rope, tape, few glasses of preserves but no bags. He interrupted Rebecca I have to ask but you know where the bags usually are. Oh yes Travis moved them there to the top cabinets. Nathan grabbed a few bags but his mind never left the lower cabinets. He laid the bags upon the table stuffing the food inside. How many you think we'll need Rebecca asked. I suggest we'll need 3 more I'd hate to be in the middle of the week and we're back out here. He turned back to the cabinet grabbing the rope and tape leaving the door open. Carefully walking over to Rebecca, he pauses a moment questions himself unfamiliar awkwardness.

She was bent into the refrigerator arranging the shelves. She raises back into the folds of Nathans arms wait, wait, wait what's going on she yelled? Nathan said "I have a treat for you we're about to get to it in a minute. He applied so much pressure around her neck that she was unable to move, it cut her breath off. Her eyes began to close, he released his arms a little. "No sleep for you" She was particularly more desirable to him, the rush of grabbing her had taken over him to the point of no control. He had lost it, he was more unfocused than he had ever been. He felt himself had come alive, you've induced my happiness you've just given me more than any woman this far licking the side of her face. Rebecca reached backwards squirming swinging confused as she begins to cough she mumbled, what's going on? Nathan had no idea, no plan, he held her for a moment... Aww yea that's what we'll do he said. Looking up at the rafters in the ceilings of the lodge.

It was still silent behind the walls it was the solitude he needed to carry out what he was about to do.

He pulled her backward toward the center of the floor. Placing his leg in front of hers pushing her toward the floor he yelled, "don't move, I dare you." Now he places his knee across her shoulders near her neck, she screams "you're hurting me what the hell, Nathan don't do this. He replied, it's already done. It was nearest the lowest point of the lodge he was holding the rope and tape in one hand. He dropped the tape to the floor while slinging the rope over the rafters catching the loose end and pulling it down, he made a knot around one hand pulling her arms toward the front of her connecting the two and double looping around both wrists. Aww what are you doing fuck, fuck let me go. While Rebecca was trying to break free, Nathan shouted, what are you doing? He puts his large knee across her shoulder preventing her from moving, he grabbed the tape and taped her mouth her mumbles could be heard while he grabbed the rope from above. Pulling against her aggressively tying one hand then the other.

You shouldn't have tempted me, you know what you're doing. She couldn't make a sound but eyes showed the look of fear and confusion. Now both hands rising pulling her upright, you're going to love this, you little filthy bitch. He secures the rope stretching her arms upward she was nearly on the tip of her toes. After she was secure he heads back to the cabinet to retrieve more rope and a knife. Taking the rope tossing it over the rafters behind them one to the right the other to the left. Reaching to grab Rebecca leg as she kicks and it was too much for Nathan he pauses and looks. I'm going to get this fucking rope on you if it's the last thing I do, grabbing her leg again and attempts by quickly putting her ankle between his knees locking it in place. Lifting the other attaching it to the rope to the right side then the other with the left now suspended in mid-air she dangles. look at you all that kicking for nothing. Now let's see what to do with all this he grabs the knife her eyes bulk unsure what was going on. Rub it over her chest. would you look at that those precious melons. Collaring her shirt taking the knife jaggedly cutting down the middle into her bra. The sleeves followed she was topless her breast hung. You think I want them you're a dirty slut who likes teasing men. I've heard all about you they say you don't like giving it up. He then unfastens her pants she still tries to yank free in mid-air. Rebecca save your dramatics you'll hang there until I set you free. I really didn't want to do this. I've tried to avoid it but you! You've earned this, I'll teach you to never walk around in front of me like this. I've been patient with you see if you like this. He begins to hit her over and over and over again she screams but her voice is muffled. Say you like it. So, you like it. mundoo mmmdoo mmmmmmmm.mmmmmmm. mmm I can't imagine what was going through her head. And her breast swings in mid-air her feet dangle with her legs wide open. She was exposed imagine the humidity. Nathan beats her for a while although she couldn't yell she could smell the stink of his breath. His powerful hands coming down with all his force her flesh rattled, leaving marks that appeared to have blood coming from them. After he finished he cut her loose one leg then the other followed by her hands spanking each one. Both feet now on the floor she stands. He grabs her by the face and tells her, if you tell anybody I will bring you back out here and beat you more. It wasn't sex that he wanted, it was those things that he suffered as a child passed down. He was now what his father was to his sisters no one ever knew. No one even cared to ask Nathan drinking was partly the effect of his earlier childhood abuse. Most of the times he had to stand there and watch his sister get beat in that same manner. He hid it well it was the first time he ever reacted on responses. It wouldn't be the last well at least his intentions to be the last. Everything that Rebecca thought of him was lost within that time, she respected him as a man and she felt as if he respected her the same. If someone had told her daddy had these issues she would argue that those things didn't exist within him. Now he's face-to-face with Rebecca removing the tape removing the Rope allowing her to see again. She looks at the floor a shame she stands there naked. He humiliated her he took a part of her that he couldn't replace. He took her virtue her happiness her ability to love to trust. A monster within her someone who would be unable to forgive. Never to trust another soul. He stood there and told her go grab some a Bertha's things or something that looks decent so when we return to the house Travis won't notice. Avoid Travis go to your room before you go to bed take a long hot soak in warm water. Nathan walked over to the door looking out of it. It was still just silent as it was when they entered. He turns and look at Rebecca I'll be in the house and remember don't you dare say a word. She sat down on the floor and cried profusely she had never been more sadden or felt that much pain. She said to herself I'll get you back I'll get you back, you no good fuck "why would you do this to me "she said to herself. She stood up walked over to Bertha's things remembering her words treat everybody in accordance to how they treat you. It was as she almost lost control of her person. Within this short span of time she gained control of herself again. She dressed in Bertha's favorite shirt she wore often around the house. There was a pair of her own pants left from working out in the yard. She put those on and headed to the door as she was walking out she looked too the Stars, she thought to herself and the world you're so beautiful why is there so much pain. She questioned God she held her head up she didn't want to remember so she put it to the back of her mind. She went into the house there was no sign of Nathan, or Travis she tiptoed to her room. Finding something fresh to put on she searched in pain finding fresh garments then to draw a bath. Adding alcohol for a long soak. She fell asleep during her soak awaken hoping it was just a dream it wasn't this was the reality.

She never spoke a word of it, she never even looked at Nathan again for some time to come. She avoided him at all costs. Travis never even paid attention he continued his daily obligations going to work coming home. Rebecca carried on high responsibilities as she always did. Always leaving Nathan his dinner in the microwave.

Months had passed it was around the holidays., it was a Saturday morning Rebecca was in the kitchen fixing breakfast. Nathan called out to her, Rebecca he shouts. He had not spoken to her in months that could only mean one thing. She pondered she paced the floor thinking to herself. She looked around thought about a knife she thought about the hot boiling water on the stove it would have been too much. She only thinks of punishing him the way he punished her. She waited closed her eyes and gracefully walked toward the door, she touched the doorknob, paused and took a deep breath, and sighed. She cracked the door she saw the tip of his feet the blanket was barely pulled up over him lying there in gym shorts. It was just her luck. She turned and walked away from the door she was to leave him. It was her chance she became vindictive the rage return with anger.

I got you now just lay there and wait I's coming right in. Rope over her shoulder and tape in her hand. She wore low rider jeans, strap stuck in the back of her pants.

Easily sneaking in once again.

Nathan laid with his toes pointing to the ceiling. Rebecca walks over kneeling at the end of the bed easing the rope around his ankle tying it's end to the bottom of the bed.

She made several loops ensuring the tightness

He was drunken sleep moving periodically to arrange his position. Rebecca whispers motherfucker don't you dare wake up I got your ass now. Extending the rope to the side of the bed looping it around his other foot. Pulling to cause his legs to open wider. Rebecca takes the rope under the bed tightening by pulling against it. Nathan hands rested on his body, Nathan laying there still snoring she lifts his hands looping them together, reaching for something on his nightstand to lock them together she grabs a large candle puts it between his hands and ties it tight Nathan awakes as she ties and pulls it tighter.

Nathan What the fuck you doing crazy bitch

Rebecca you called did you? I'm going to show you crazy Bitch lay there!

You thought I was going to let you get away with that. You thought you was crazy I'm crazy

. She took the tape wrapped it around his head, mouth tying several ways over the rope. Nathan laid restraint looking mumbling. He laid yanking and pulling trying to break free. How does it feel?

Rebecca left the room wrote a note hanging it on the door. I'm in town just in case Travis was to come home she then ran into the bathroom looking for alcohol to pour on him awhile she attempts to bludgen him. Moving bottles around she came across a container of warming cream. Oh, bitch you about to get it she said (A look of vengeance on her face speedily returning to the room closing the door behind her. Now you were calling me, I believe you were planning on putting your nasty stinking dick in my mouth weren't you.

Rebecca leaned over struggle to pull his pants down. Aww look at that he's not so big and bad without you being in control. Let me get it up for you. "You're going to love this" Rebecca Straddled one of his legs rubbing the cream up his body. She replied it's about to get hot in here for real. Let me make you feel good I've had the greatest teacher.

Grabbing the warming cream, she started at his feet rubbed it up his legs even rubbed it on his privates. She continues to rub it up his chest until his whole body was covered. Are you warm yet, that ass is about to burn up in here. She then commenced to beating continuously yelling no good bastard, stupid fuck how did you think that you were going to beat me. What kind of men do this s***. She took special interest in beating his genitals.

Say you like it! she said, confused he laid Mumbled I like it as she reached for the warming cream. Placing it in her hand grabbing his penis stroking it up and down Rebecca gets up and wait minutes by now he's starting to burn mumble and scream. She grabbed the strap swinging it again toward his shaft repeating hitting it whilst he struggles burning and stinging. She stops, placing some on his balls ..oops I drop some she carefully places and pack some near his anus. This should really get you moving she begins beating him all over ending with the bottom of his feet. She says to him if you ever touch or look at me again or anyone else you'll get the same thing again. He laid there squirming as she cuts the ropes he was bruised from head to toe. She ends by dashing alcohol over him you simple minded bitch. Get up get you a bath stinking drunk ass, belittling him as she left the room. Proudly holding her head up carefully watching. Travis didn't get in until late that night doing his usual sitting on the porch thinking about his future life to come. The next day came Nathan was barely walking and getting around. Rebecca and Travis sitting at the table eating breakfast, "How are you this morning, Rebecca says. He mumbles under his breath stupid bitch. Rebecca gets up steps on his feet. Aww shit you stepped on my feet. Excuse me I didn't mean to. Travis looked at them and noticed a slight tension while continuing to eat his breakfast. The time Nathan remained there was quiet and peaceful he never so much as looked at Rebecca again. Shame of what she had done to him or what he had done to her both where off limits to each other.

Years had passed Travis had worked enough adding money to his account from his mother's insurance policy and the selling of the cleaners. He had saved just enough to start his travel agency which was now a working success.

Life was ordinary nothing rarely happened outside the occasional travelers stopping in which made his business a success. People of their town was always willing to travel & see different things. But Travis himself never took advantage of his own vacations but knew of the places that where best to travel.

When things where slow he took the time to look out the window. On one particular, sunny morning he noticed a young lady sitting on the curb across the street. He stared sipping his coffee returning to his work preparing packages for travelers. Mid-day soon came it was time for lunch Rebecca was headed out the door. Where are you going for lunch? oh I left something back home, hammy and cheese I fixed earlier this morning besides Bishop is waiting on me I must fix him something to. It's really starting to get old. Travis replied, you'll be fine you're strong enough. Oh, sounds good, I'll just run up the street to the diner and grab something. Travis proceeded to the car once again looking across the street. He noticed the young lady from earlier was still there now inside the car looks to be asleep. Walking over to the car thinking questions himself. This could be a crazy person and here I go walking over to get attacked alerted of his presence she raises. Here we go! How are you I noticed you've been sitting here for some time? I didn't want to leave without checking on you. I'm fine you can go about your day thanks. Travis turned and turned again facing the lady walking closer. I mean no harm just checking on your wellbeing. Look I don't mean to be rude but as I've stated I'm fine. Travis walked away to his car headed up to the diner up the street. He had his regular soup with warm cornbread his wonders carried him back to his conversation with the young lady he'd met. He looked around the diner wanting to go back and secure the conversation offering an apology. Travis call the waiter over, he was a normal customer she replied by name. Can I get anything else for you Travis? Why yes you can what's the most common usual most enjoy? Most people enjoy the sausage with rice gravy we sell a lot of it she looks at Travis with a bewildering face. He always orders the same things. I'll have that to go. Ok I'll have your order up in minutes.

Travis awaited thinking again about how she may respond, she brings his order he proceeds back to the office

Walks over this time she's leaned against the hood. Travis walks over I don't mean to bother you I think we got off on the wrong foot. I went out for lunch and I thought you may be hungry you've been over here for hours. She stared without returning a voice May I ask of you your name please. Next, you'll ask my name and begin to talk I know your kind. My kind? Travis paused what kind would that be may I ask. Her spirits where lifted confessed I'm Christina and thank you. I'm just having a bad day and not use to people approaching me. Travis walked over passing the food that was prepared at the diner passing it alone to her.

He began to show concern and an eagerness to know what it was she was having difficulty with. Not to add my problems to your day influencing any affection to myself of you.

I've left home my boyfriend is over baring and abusive I'm unsure of what I need to do so I'm sitting here trying to figure it out. Travis sat on the ground she never looked down at him she begins to spill over in comfortable repeats. I don't know what to do. Hey!! Wait thanks for taking the time to come over to check on me. Meeting you has been a better part of my day it's hard to use these words. It's been so long since I've seen a man that I can appreciate. With all due respect, not just to myself but all women, hope that you will remain this way. Most importantly I need friends like you Thank you don't be afraid to speak now you've fed me now you've earned my continuous conversation. Oh, it's like that? just that easy, he chuckled. Thanks for the compliment, I just noticed that you were sitting and want to know if I could help. I've had my share of bad days part of my life it seems that's all there were. I must say had you met me years ago you'd sat near me just like this. Christina goes on to say well the bigger of my problem is I fell in love with a man who hasn't been all that great for my life.

I thought that I had found a purpose with him he addressed me with beautiful thoughts every day. He woke me in the morning with thing that rattle my understanding these things held me. I thought we were lovers turns out he was just another guy wanting to pimp me. Pimp you? Travis urgently replies Yes pimp me. I had never gone out with anyone like him. I'm just putting you all in my business.

I should have responded before you left. I can't express to you enough how sorry I am and how bad I feel about that. I was forced into this life now that I'm here I'm not sure if I love or regret it. Travis stood pondering, so what is it exactly that you do for him? I noticed you said pimp which usually implies that there's an exchange for money or sort. Help me understand I'm not exactly a modern-day house wife. I'm literally a prostitute I go out at nights to resolve our financial issues. I done it because he'd said so. now I think I love it with great interest. I never saw myself in this light, I've held these secrets to long everyone had other expectations and high hopes for me being what they wanted for me. The only issues I have with this is

I'm constantly hiding from myself lying to others. Again, Travis saw no reason to stop her from talking he sat there and listen with his hands wrapped around his knees. She ate and spoke in length about her experiences. He believes this was by far the realest conversation he had with anyone, never heard such indifference. Although it was taking away from his work he allowed time to pass looking past everything he was used to. It was no imaginary story and was excepting as it was interesting. He was a shame he had no stories to tell, at that moment he realized he hadn't lived. Wow.

wow intrigued and stumbling over his words he now needed to know what it was like. I can't imagine I really can't, I know it's alone the same lines of honestly, I don't know what to say beside apologize for his mistakes.

What do you do if you're with someone you're no longer wanting to be with? Christina carried on I care for him I believed it was something real connecting us. I don't want to be with him and I'm scared to tell him because he keeps threatening me. I've no kids so I hurt to think time has been wasted. I just don't feel it with him anymore. I don't like this relationship I've endured much, now time to do something different. Travis paused the conversation, oh perhaps we can finish this later I have a few things reserved awaiting me

She was now relaxed in the mind ridding mental disorders ready to begin life at the pace where she had stopped

Will you always be here she carried on. Yes, he replied ended it with a warm hug that help improve her condition walking across back to his office.

Rebecca greeted him oh, I see have we made new friends? Travis smiled, maybe! replied in conjunctions over work divided by his recent conversation he had with Christina. Bishop wanted you to come by the house when you got the time. Oh yes of course! How has he been. Rebecca he's been fine the usual complaints can't get him to go outside anymore. I just let him sit on the couch in front of the TV. There's no enthusiasm and I have not the strength to keep both of us going.

Bishop was her fiancé when they first met he was full of life ambitious and very outgoing. He was ready to take on the world until.

On the way home from a business trip he and a colleague was in a car accident that took his sight. Bishop was the lucky one his colleague lost his life he was a mentor to Bishop.

They had the type of friendship where they did everything. Their wives or fiancé's cooked together. Invite each other to family dinners spent nights on the town together. They made great memories, after the accident all those things changed his colleague's wife moved back home where her family was. The friendship was no longer as it once was so Bishop drowned in his own misery.

Most everything he needed Rebecca had to do it, there were very few things he could do for himself. Work came to an end that day. He went by Rebecca's to see Bishop to chat with him for a while and left. Bishop said Travis next time I see you I have some things I need to get off my chest.

Travis was his only support team and nowhere else to turn at the time. Rebecca said, we are going out tonight I guess just to get out I assume.

Travis was occupied with thoughts of Christina. Reflecting over his chat every night curious about what Christina life was like. What must it take to elevate the mind to reduce its eagered morals he thought. Distance bonds that secured their newly found friendship. She thought of his charm and he interest himself in her life as well simultaneously.

They both longed to taste of each other more so to see each other Christina found it surprising she would think of someone biting on her neck.

Who knew that this would be what inspired a friendship not yet formed. Somehow Travis knew what we wanted of her

Their stories differed but in meeting their souls collided showing kindness to both and figuring out what each needed. He knew there was wanted feelings of affection she was just the right height perfect skin tone and held a smile that glows ... Both considered carefully about what it was the other wanted. Just as Travis walked into his office there was a knock on the door.

Some time had passed Travis wondered when he'd be seeing her. Drawn to her with intensity. He had thought about her for days wondered what spending time with her was like. It was that particular knock that ignited his heart again. From the moment, I laid eyes on you it was the breath of life that your presence took me by surprise he said. And here you are again. You're a flawless part of my imagination I couldn't have conceived. We talked the other day those moments I can't let go ...How comfortable you made me feel. I waited for you to reappear it was like forever. It was later that evening Bishop and Rebecca night out. They arrived at their Destination she began to look out the window she aww wow. Bishop you shouldn't have I've never heard if this place before how you ahhh. In response, he said I heard it was amazing and from the looks of things it is grabbing her hand can you tell me what it looks like she began to tell him. The trees align up across the yard with twinkling lights inside of them. Walk ways are stained oak each had paths that looped around them. There are fenced lights hanging perfectly a line chandelier made of Marquez cut glass just gorgeous. And there's a fountain with bedding of flowers around it water with lights installed that changes the colors while moving about. Bishop takes a step forward; can you take me over by the fountain I want to feel the splashes of water against my face. It sounds so amazing the water has its own tune as beautiful as it looks the sound is incredibly amazing. They walk by the fountain soon. As the first drop of water touches him Bishop drops down to one knee reaching for Rebecca's hand. She stands there amazed looking and impressed turning to him as he holds a ring in his hand on one knee. Ahhh. what are you doing Bishop? Bishop noo noo. nooo. nooo. Bishop please noo. shhhhh. shhh hh. Rebecca may I introduce you to a new life that consist of you putting your emotional needs in a place where they can be safe. I'm offering you this out of love in hopes that it becomes our way of understanding. I want to live a life balanced between the two of us in accord with this pledge asking your hand to join me in marriage. I heard you say no when you saw me in this position what you are saying no you don't want to or no from being excited. Bishop I love you I'm willing to do whatever you want. Yet marriage is a big step I'm not ready to consider I know how you feel about me I appreciate it I don't want you to feel less because I'm saying no. Bishop stands well ok I'll give you more time to think about it but I need to ask why. To be honest Bishop if I'm to marry you it comes with responsibilities I'm not ready to commit my life to. Even now I have issues of not being able to do some of the things. I consider being as part of a relationship. I want kids and can't imagine what that would be like. Rebecca I'm aware of all these things but I won't try to convince you that I'm what u need in your life. Your what I want and I was under the impression none other would do. However, this changes everything I've given you my whole heart nothing less I'm without sight but I'm not without feeling or compassion. Let's not dwell on this let's enjoy this moment

They enjoyed their time but bishop couldn't get past it. He left it alone the following day. Rebecca at the office debating over letting her relationship go. But soon interrupted with allowing Christina in to visit Travis. Delighted

Good morning Travis, blushing Christina showed up at his office without warning, do you always have the right words for strangers. She chuckled aloud. Anyways I was going through my mental notes I came across you. I'm aware of your hectic schedules and know time is limited for you. I'm to wonder if you're willing to sacrifice some time for me. Time is precious with you it is also valuable. Can I repay you for the other day coffee, dinner, breakfast you choose? But don't cheat us. You've made my past days beautiful earning my presence. When you want our need hopefully you feel that same.

Travis replied there are many things that I'm unaware of I want to learn and understand. There will always be something that I might not like but it helps me learn and understand who I'm becoming I've not had many relationships. In the sense of being friends or otherwise close to anyone besides my mother and Rebecca. They've been my company threw out life. Although my mother is dead she left me with many things to think about. The relationship of her and my father had to be something magical she spoke of with such grace. Christina continues well what will it be?

Ok I can stand a night out on the town with you.

Travis was excited how should I dress, how you feel comfortable Christina said. Find a more relaxed part of yourself dress to look good. The Clock Was ticking it was almost time for them to go. Travis got dressed in all white trousers and loafers a button up white-collar shirt with a tan sports jacket it was different attire for him. He got in the car proceeded to meet Christina. He pulled up to local Tavern he was in the car looking around nervous wondering what time she would arrive. He noticed across the street in the back alley there was a car sitting only marker lights on. He thought it to be strange, what he didn't know was Christina was in the car she is carrying on her nightly affairs. Travis gave no attention to the car he sat watching. There were three women all dressed differently from what he'd seen. The first one wore laced 6-inch heels with black leather shorts with a top had to be made of rayon. Her hair was black with yellow tints. She carried a purse in which she frequently looked inside. The second had on a red top and white bottom flat shoes. And the last had short hair and an all over fitted dress with 4-inch heels. Travis was out of his element with everything going on around him. There he sat in front of the Tavern looking. You'd think the three drunken guys standing out arguing over a simple pool game would bother him. Or the couple who were getting high in the car next to him while lights were flashing. Travis only wondered how he would be able to talk to the three young ladies that had walked across the street now in front of him. He was sure that they spoke Ebonics and he didn't know a word of it. He was intrigued, listening to Christina story he wanted to speak to more people such as her. He got out of the car leaning against it. He was a score for a trick and didn't know it. One of the girls paid close attention, she walked over hey Daddy you looking to have some fun. Poor Travis why yes, I am. But I'm waiting for a friend and she responded how are you going to have fun waiting on someone else. I'm all the fun that you need. He had no idea what she was referring to. She grabbed his hand where you want to go he responded ahhhh... Wherever you go to have fun. Okay get in the car. Travis walked back around to the driver door he got in, she got in on the other side she proceeded to lean over grabbing his zipper to his pants. Wait what are you doing, by that time Christina's walking up out the alley. Yelling across the street bitch if you don't get your trick ass up out of that car I'm going to knock a hole in the top of your mutherfucking head with your raggedy ass. Get the fuck out now he's no trick. She turned and looked at Christina what the fuck. What is he a cop or something. No, he's my date, bitch there's nothing going on around here.

You either tricking or hustling looks to me he's not doing either. But then I guess he gets a pass today. Next time he come around he got to pay. You must want that mutherfucking wig snatched off your head, I'm going to tell you one time get the fuck on.

Travis laid beside Christina

I'm a man flawed but have something to offer people of my choosing. There's nothing better than giving besides friendship or just being real with others. I'd like to have those moments back it wasn't enough. I want to be engulfed in your passions.

If I could have you I'd kiss you slower, I'd massage your body, I'd slowly bite you on your ass, I'd suck and lick on your nipples, I'd rub on your clit make you cum much as you want, I'd make you cum more than once, more than twice I'd hold you and listen to you talk. These are the things that I want. Recap I'd do it all over again and again and again. You're my sexual satisfaction. I didn't know what I wanted until I saw you. I hope to taste desserts off your skin like strawberries off your nipples and cherries off your cherry. Matter of fact if you have time I want to hear you moan in my ear and hopefully we can reach satisfaction together. I don't want to waste time just talking.

Christina responds, shit man

I have fantasies that should have long been lived out. None that appealed to me or caught my attention till you came alone. I previously thought about somethings just as love but dismissed that ideas.

I never thought to feel for anyone but this guy that beats me taking my money. Travis, I want you but this life keeps me.

Christina help me to understand you because I can't be helped by only me to understand myself. Maybe you remind me of myself in a lot of ways. I've asked myself why would you be my lover. Then again look at you so amazingly wonderful. Most women would love to be on your arms. I'd just love to be in your company as much as possible you give life meaning for me.

Travis

I had already made love to you it wasn't the hands it was the comfort of mind the peace shared between us. It's these things you feel giving and receiving it's just special with taste and bites. You've not said but you've envisioned me in multiple ways. How many times you've discovered yourself? I know what I give to you and why. I'll make you carry extra panties along with you. I have thought of u in many ways.

Christina

Listening to you share things has made me care deeply I hope you can be happy knowing I'm with him for now. I'm here whenever you need me. Meaning I want you to be comfortable I'll share myself with you all you can have. I'll need that much more in return you're so dam interesting I can't even tell you what I'd be willing to do for you. I can't wait until you're ready for all of this.

Christina take Travis out to a nearby lake. The house was well-lit it had stone walk ways mostly of marble. The drapes were pulled back he could see everything within the home. It was bright. You could see custom antiques from outside. It was a place she was quite comfortable she told stories of growing up there. This was news to Travis it was her grandmother's home she took him by the hand walking up to the door entered." In the Foyer set a large mirror oh wow Travis said this is very nice. Yes, everything in this home is my grandmother's we wanted to leave it just like it was after her passing. She was sweet and contrive let alone she was admired by many. Her role in the community was very significant she worked in a text Parra's office I'm unsure of her duties. It must have been very important nevertheless we're here and I like to show you my favorite room. It was my room as a little girl now it's vacant I never got a chance to have company in here actually you'll be the first guy to enter this room. Travis standing amazement of how a house of this age could be so gorgeous. High gloss wooden floors super white walls with chandeliers in each room assortment of antique furniture. There was a stairway curved painted white with a wooden banister. They walked up the stairs. There was soft music playing coming from a room down the hall in the direction and which they were going. They came up to the door Travis admired the antique knob noticing the flower petals lying against wooden stained floors at the bottom of the door. She always kept the room in a romantic setting. Christina opened the door. She asked him to remove his shoes leave them by the door. Christina walked about the room to her nightstand removing her earrings letting her hair down. As Travis walks over kissing her on the shoulder. Wrapping his arms around her waist they begin swaying to the music. Gently pulling her hair back he kissed her neck. She gasps grabbing onto his hands exhaling. Travis what are you doing, she slightly pulls away a little looking at him you know the things that I do. You know that I go back home to him. Christina, I can't help myself I need you in my life I want you like I've never wanted another woman. I can't bare the thought of not having you in my world. I want this us, would you be willing to be as you are. Just give me what I need of you. There was a king size bed golden in color hand carved silk gray headboard. Beautiful it was with a black silk comforter laid with golden pillows. I'd like to freshen up for you wait for me. He waits gazing into the darkness over the lights around the lawn looking down the street. There was nothing to be seen for miles he found himself to be blissful. Running his fingers over the back of a king chair that sat near the window. He unbuttons his shirt laying it over the back of the chair, placing his watch on the table nearby he wanted to be ready for her. He was in deep thought questioning how he felt and why he felt so strongly attracted to her. He never experienced anything like it, what would people think came cross his mind but he soon brushed that out of his mind. After a while Christina walks back in the room. He never heard the door open, she walks over Travis still looking out the window she places her hands on his back rubbing downwardly placing her hands around him laying her head on his shoulders "you make me feel so good." Her hair graces his body. He grabs her hands and pulls her closer, you make me feel so good.

Do u think you'll ever love again hypocritically he questioned. Or are you capable of a relationship that is serious. I'm asking because after prior relationships we lose pieces of ourselves.

Christina, I think so. I can't let one relationship steal my joy.

Travis, you're a true romantic, but do I ever cross your mind?

Christina, yes anyone willing to dance with no music just to be in motion. I can't help but allow my thoughts to follow.

They smiled.

Travis you've allowed yourself to smile when you're angry with me. I have many questions as u can see but I hope to have forever to ask. Love me patiently, allow others to be kind and respect that without it being confused with a weakness. I have so many hopeless thoughts of how our love should be yet you may not understand maybe it's the dreams that invade my reality that I'd love to see fulfilled. My desires without intentions just to be near you sharing ideas. Chattering about senseless things that bring about smiles, watching suns set as stars sparkle in your eyes. Listen to the magic of words rearranging what was to and what will come. Maybe it can be special. I'm just excited about us right here right now.

Travis on his knees easing down to lay flat. Alignment with her body
allowed him to take his tongue in and out of her opening replacing it

Travis counter step backwards, turns to face her, petals align his feet
some between his toes. He backed over pulling her hand until his leg hit
the bed. He was holding both hands he releases one, pulling her around
to the bed. She turns unzipping her night gown hair flows from a mild
breeze flowing from a nearby window. He watches her body reveal
itself her long leg were very well shaded. He could only visualize his lips
pressed against her skin. Her body was curved in right proportions. I can
only imagine what she must have felt like beneath him. It felt magical
their breaths were in tune with each other. He set her on the bed. Laid
her back begin at her feet rubbing placing her toes in his mouth, she
twitched. The breeze worked in his favor since her toes were wet. Her
eyes closed immediately. She whispered you don't have to, he slowly
kisses up her thighs, she grabs the sheets nervously anticipating each
move. Taking her hand to his head imagine what he felt it was his reality
from the things that he seen. It was the only place he wanted to be. It
was something she often thought of to be wanted the way she wanted
another. To be caressed and to feel loved. The aroma and fragrance of
her body was so sweet to him he couldn't help himself. He released his
tongue down her thigh nibbling, he feels her body quiver. Grazing over
her pubic area making lines downwardly she instantly becomes wet. He
then runs his tongue up alongside her clitoris. He began to vibrate his
tongue back and forth slowly along with the up-and-down motion. He
sucks on it, he gets carried away growling placing his whole mouth on
it, treating it as if he has never been with a woman before. She was the
delicacy for his pallet. She releases again, Travis makes a slurping sound
nawing, moving his head from left to right round about in a circular
motion. Holding on to and pulling apart her ass cheeks squeezing and
jiggling them increasing pleasures. Her moans filled the room she was
in a panicking state gasping Oh Travis. ooooh my ooooh my she could
hear the sounds of him licking her. Shiiiiiittt... Travis. The bed felt like
a place she wanted to be forever. Open wider for me he said. Lifting and
spreading her legs wider so he could have more of her.

Travis on his knees easing down to lay flat. Alignment with her body
allowed him to take his tongue in and out of her opening replacing it

with his fingers. Now sucking on her clitoris again he milks her G spot. He wanted to feel her large releases. He wanted to please her as no one could. The bed got drenched, taking his time, she began to get wetter and wetter. He nawls with his teeth soft bites... She releases trying to escape him he holds on intensifying her pleasure. Planting her feet in his back Travis uses this as leverage raising up lowering her. Hold on don't move your legs. Now on his knees he unbuttons his pants all she could hear was the sound of his zipper and the wrestling of his clothes. Pulls them halfway down he was bulged and erected. Pulls his shaft out he was impressed with the veins in it, runs his hands down it a few strokes he takes notices to how he'd never been so enthused. Christina holding on as he pulls her body back down to the bed opening her legs wider, looking at the wetness, runs the head of his penis up and down her split, the glistening of her cum gives him the pleasure of sight right before he shoves it in she releases more.

Their bodies collide she reaches he pulls it was almost like heaven he looks into her eyes she in his. The second a stroke was so slow they both trembled. He felt the warmth closing in. She tightens her muscles making her body flex with his. Don't nut don't nut I want to have it ..Baby please can I have it she said arousing him even more his thrust became long strokes. He wanted her to feel all of him. She pulled him closer on top of her rolling him over, it came out she places one hand on his chest sides it back in her with the other. The pleasures of her sliding down on it was defined as a great leaning toward over on him twirling her ass rubbing her clit. Travis hands tightens his body stiffened awwww...ahhhh. they both begin to cum.

Travis laid drunken and sexed crazed talking

I can be wild 4 you...

Give you lashes if that's what you want you could have.

Toes for breakfast while looking at your

Delicious lips wet and waiting...

Allow my fingers a taste you

Moan in your ear to start a fire...

Spankings?

Let me strap up come get it again.

I see you needing a good one

I could be freaky but I just want to watch...

Tie your legs while you

Getting your ass licked

Just for the expressions

Don't you want to beg, get on your knees…

Needing someone to play with I see your

Nipple harder than ever choose one...

You can have them all

They laughed

On the next morning Travis reflected over his night out with Christina and was pleased with all the things he had experienced. Yet he pondered about the connection in the relationship what would be her purpose and his willingness to disclose more of his life to her. Laying there thinking time slipped away noticing it was near 7:30 it was too late to go for his morning run so he jumped into action got dressed hurriedly. Travis headed to the office once he arrived the lady from the other day awaited him. HI Travis Remember me Jill from the other day my husband and I came into the office to book a trip? I was returning because our pass ports finally arrived and wanted to rearrange the dates a little. OH, that's fine come on in I've had a long night you must forgive my presence, I'm neither together or myself this morning. Just give me a few minutes and make yourself at home. I'll be starting up some coffee I'd like to offer you some if you're a drinker. Her response was humorously delighting. Watching Travis roam around the office lost was pleasing for her to see. I do believe that I'd enjoy that, how long have you been in business in this office. I've only recently noticed it after looking for the nail shop down the street. Travis laughed it makes sense to have the perfect nails while on vacation if you don't mind my saying so the rest of you is so well put together. Travis had always been forward at a speaking he wondered to himself how the words were able to roll off his tongue as they did. Continuing I noticed that the other day. Jill smiled blushed even harder thank you for noticing compliments are far and few now days. The strangest look came across Travis face, by that what do you mean any man with eyes can see that you're a very stylish woman. A very good looking one if I may add. Well you see there is where the problem is, I am more than a look I have qualities that are often times over looked. I've been cursed with this beauty I feel somedays men only talk to me for two reasons either they're attracted to me or they are insecure about themselves. Wow...I've never heard such a thing wherever did you come to that conclusion. Most women would love to own your beauty or your charm. Travis shuffles his papers and remove his coffee off the heating pot pours up her cup. Well Travis to be honest most people can't possibly understand what it's like being in the presence of people who only wants you for what they see. When I'm set aside and praised for my beauty I feel distance from what I'm able to provide a person with. There's an emptiness that comes over me no real connection of human instinct. Even at home with the man I'm married to he never really see me he sees my flesh. He desires my flesh more than he desires my conversation. Sometimes I'm lonely even when I'm around groups of people. The people that are not there for loving what or who I am spend time wasting on ways trying to break parts of me. Wanting to see how I may react to certain thing find my weakness just insults my intelligence. That's an amazing take on life. Travis agrees, when did you discover all of this I'd normally disagree but I understand it all too well. Never have I viewed it with so much depth. To understand what you're going through is almost like second nature to me. I've experience most of it myself but on a different accord to want to exist in people lives and they never see the inside of you. Their eyes will never allow them to position themselves beside you. This only means the conversations will never be on the same level because of something within them makes them feel guilty. Guilty! What do you mean Travis? I've lead this conversation but now I'm lost. Well it's like this we all as you know have flaws but some more than others. In some people lives they feel less than human embarrassment from the way they look shapes forms and disadvantages. Overall, they have to deal with these things on a daily basis it's a never-ending cycle mirrors are just reminders. They are so focused on what's not so perfect and never see the perfection of the gift inside. Some have gifts so extraordinary that no one would ever look at their face. No one view their bodies just to try to find insight of what type of person they are dealing with. The intellectual experience that would be so receptive turns the mind to attention instead of the eyes to details. When they view you, they see themselves and the difference. We can make resentfully, despise any actions you may take to better yourself or even just to be normal around our peers. Travis continue please, you're on a roll here, you said that with so much passion do you mentor in your spare time it's a lot of people out there could really use the things your saying. Maybe if they could understand and see life a little better. Well I'm not the mentoring type this is just my take on it. After the passing of my mother I experience the world around me filled with so much greed and jealousy. My tears where of no matters to the people around me. My tears shedded alone had me to wonder why life had taken me down a path with no one to listen. I would get people to listen with their ears but no one listened with a heart, to adhere my truest needs.

People became so blind everyone say let them have peace. Truth is I never wanted to be alone. It's like they forgot what I was going through because they indirectly felt my pain or experience the trauma of my emotions. Doesn't mean I wanted to be reminded I took all the hurtful things that was said towards me and my mother and put it all into my master piece which is where we sit and talk today. It was all my mother talked about owning her own travel agency. This gave me the powerful meaning of pleasure to myself. Travis I'm so thankful someone shares insight to the way I've seen somethings I try telling this to my husband but he has this one-sided view as to maybe I look to far into things. Speaking of which where is your girlfriend from the other day Christina I believe her name was. Christina is not to be perceived as my girlfriend she's someone I met the same day you and your husband came in. I only met her hours before the two of you walked through the door. She's also a very enlightening person I'm rather fun of but we are too far different. When we meet people we never know what to expect as you and I have been sitting chatting and gotten off the topic of getting your trip ready is the same way she and I got off on the right foot. I'm guilty of allowing good people to getting next to me, most of the times it's my own fault. I truly have a sense of humanity for people.

Travis if I didn't have no one to be with I'd look for men such as yourself.

Jill and Travis where interrupted by Rebecca, she wanted to know if the paperwork for tickets were ready. Smiling knowing the conversation had to be exciting from the expression Travis on are you finished with the paperwork no he responded. I'm just about to wrap things up as we speak set the cup coffee down on the- collector hurt thing headed to the door may I walk you out in a generally gentlemanly fashion. He walked her to the door opened the door she collected her things.

that will cover you in any belief that one day we shall meet and smile together. Allow laughter to become our only language.

Rebecca gets a phone call, it was bishop Honey what time can I expect you.

Bishop if you allow me to finish I'll be in there shortly to help you out.

Oh, dear I didn't want anything I was calling to see if you wanted to go out with me tonight. I know you've been working a lot and the responsibility dealing with me take its toll on you. I liked you to know I appreciate what you do for me. I remember a time where apologize for these things didn't matter as much. The truth of the matter things in life happen. I never meant for you to have to deal with any of it this. And sometimes it makes me feel bad as a man I can't contribute to my household as I was once able to.

Last few days I've been hurting I've thought about our beautiful beginning and where we are now. You've been distant and I can't say that I understand I only know to do what I've been doing or try to reach out to do a little bit better. I have to say I forgive you for your thoughts. I know there's a possibility that they haven't been pure. This has changed all of us not just you. Most of all it has taken the man you once loved Rebecca had no exchange of words, later that night.

She'd gotten dress finishing her makeup applying a fragrance. She ran down to put away her things. Running back upstairs she entered the room where Bishop was. Hey now baby, you look amazing how is it your able to know all these things and you're not able to see anything. My blindness is not my disability it's in fact the strongest part of what makes me so unique for loving you. It has allowed me to be able to appreciate what most oftentimes people like you can't. What do u mean people like me? Rebecca giggles so what do you mean the phrase "you people "Well you people that can see but have no understanding to what life is. If I'm to say not I'm not going out with Travis, you would be all bent out of shape. Wouldn't you? Your feelings would be shattered. To think that you'd be missing something where as I'd be okay with it. Doing things different! Sight can be the biggest flaw it makes the less important things a goal. Allowing the most important things to fall to the way side and holds less value. Rebecca stood with a puzzled look on her face. So, what would you consider to be important in similar circumstances. I can't tell you anything if you want to know what's important then you have to decline this night for a date with friends. Ok ill decline let me call Travis and let him know. After placing the call Bishop placed some tickets in her hand can you find this place. Let's go here tonight I hear its life changing. Oh, I believe I can. Where in heavens name you find the time to get some tickets? He responded let's just say I have my ways. Their night continued while Travis is puzzled as to why Rebecca changed her mind about meeting him after agreeing to spend the night on the town with them.

Travis went to see Bishop hey bishop it's me I'm coming in he walked in bishop came out of the room being blind numbers hard to get around it was feeling on the walls. Travis never wanted to allow him to feel helpless so he never offered help. The fact that he was his friend Travis I guess you wondering why I had you to come over. This is a strange opening for us but the game is not on my mind. It is your cousin that concerns me I proposed to her she rejected my offer. She gave me a lot of excuses but I know the truth. It hurts knowing and not being able to pretend. Travis said what's wrong. Well the problem is I was sitting in here the other day listening to the game. And I don't have to tell you that I'm blind I don't know how to say this. My hearing is excellent my touch is even better. I'm saying that to say I was on the couch watching the game please forgive me it's hard to say. And Rebecca was here she was whatever it is that you all do to prepare trips. Her phone rings! That was fine. Only a short period of time it wasn't that I was looking for anything. Moments later she told me she was going out she came over and kiss me. I heard the door close or at least I thought it closed. I heard the depths of a man's voice her whispering I even heard how they connected. The rumbling of their clothes the kisses the undoing of his pants. I heard his belt when it fell to the side. I'm to assume she had a skirt on hearing him say bend over. I know they were in the kitchen I noticed sound of a fork when it's pushed across the counter. It killed me to hear her moan silently. It only lasts a short time but it was something that I can imagine if I had sight. When they finish the door open again she announced herself. I called over to me Believe it or not I was turned on I grabbed it by hand. And I wanted her to sit on me. I wanted her even after she had been with another. I know this sound crazy. But it's the truth she pulled away from me she told me she didn't feel like it.

TO BE CONTINUED
"PRIVATE THOUGHTS INTRUSIONS"

Printed in the United States
By Bookmasters